Harlequin
Presents..

Other titles by

ANNE HAMPSON
IN HARLEQUIN PRESENTS

# 1	GATES OF STEEL
# 2	MASTER OF MOONROCK
# 7	DEAR STRANGER
#10	WAVES OF FIRE
#13	A KISS FROM SATAN
#16	WINGS OF NIGHT
#19	SOUTH OF MANDRAKI
#22	THE HAWK AND THE DOVE
#25	BY FOUNTAINS WILD
#28	DARK AVENGER
#31	BLUE HILLS OF SINTRA
#34	STORMY THE WAY
#37	AN EAGLE SWOOPED
#40	WIFE FOR A PENNY
#44	PETALS DRIFTING
#47	WHEN THE CLOUDS PART

75c each

Many of these titles, and other titles in the
Harlequin Romance series, are available at your
local bookseller, or through the Harlequin Reader
Service. For a free catalogue listing all available
Harlequin Presents titles and Harlequin Romances,
send your name and address to:

HARLEQUIN READER SERVICE,
M.P.O. Box 707
Niagara Falls, N.Y. 14302

Canadian address:
Stratford, Ontario, Canada
or use order coupon at back of books.

ANNE HAMPSON

hunter of the east

HARLEQUIN BOOKS
toronto-winnipeg

© Anne Hampson 1973

Original hard cover edition published in 1973
by Mills & Boon Limited

SBN 373-70551-4
Harlequin Presents edition published July 1974

Printed in Canada.

CHAPTER ONE

IN her hotel bedroom overlooking the Acropolis in Athens Kim Lyttleton was engaged in the happy task of wrapping a huge box of chocolates in decorative paper. Enid, one of her companions, was also busy wrapping a present, while the third member of the trio was by the dressing-table fixing a large red ribbon bow to a spray of flowers.

"Won't Mumsie be surprised!" Twisting round as she spoke, Pauline smiled at the others in turn.

"Amazed, I should say." Kim's green eyes were alight, as they invariably were in excitement or anger. "Even though we've managed, every year since we left her, to be with her on her birthday, and although we promised we always would be with her, she'll never expect that we would do it this year, not with her having come to live in Greece. She couldn't possibly have envisaged our arranging to take our annual holiday early, and together, just so we could be with her today."

"No." Enid's eyes were dreamy; she was dwelling on the past. "How lucky we were, three orphans, finding ourselves in the care of such a marvellous foster-mother."

Pauline nodded.

"Yet she used to get so vexed if we mentioned gratitude. 'I did it for the money,' she would say. 'When my husband died and left me with little Diana I applied for foster-children in order to make ends meet.' She said she'd rather do that than go out to work."

"Perhaps the money she received for us was earned a little easier than if she'd had to go out every day,

5

especially when Diana was small. Nevertheless, we were lucky; there's no doubt about that." Having finished her task Enid stood with her parcel under her arm, waiting for the others. "She's been a wonderful woman in many ways. Just imagine her having the courage to marry a Greek and come and live in a foreign country!"

"That certainly astounded me." Kim was recalling how, on a visit to her foster-mother ten months previously, she had learned of her having met a Greek, through a friend, and that she was thinking of marrying him.

"I feel the need for some adventure," Mrs. Rowe had calmly informed the disbelieving Kim. "And I think it will be an advantage to live in Greece."

"You feel the need for adventure! But, darling, you've always been such a stick-in-the mud! We could never even get you to go off on a trip to Blackpool – not without us, I mean."

"Well, I did have the four of you to look after –"

"Even when we were old enough to look after ourselves you wouldn't take a day off."

"I never liked the idea of your coming home from school and finding me out, and no tea ready, you know that. But to get back to Petros: we do have a great deal in common even though he's a foreigner, and I feel I'll be very happy with him."

"Then marry him, Mumsie." Kim knew she would miss her, but naturally she made no mention of this. "What about Diana – is she willing to go with you?"

"She likes the idea, yes."

"Will she be able to get a job there?" Six years younger than Kim, Diana had been just a little more than sixteen at the time. She was now working in her stepfather's office.

"Petros has promised her a job."

"I think," Pauline was saying, interrupting Kim's thoughts, "that it was terrifically brave of her to marry a Greek. It's said they're awful with their women."

Kim smiled.

"You do hear this, I agree, but Mumsie sounds happy enough, if her letters are anything to go by, and I expect they are. In any case, who could possibly be awful with such a darling?"

"No one," agreed Enid, glancing at her watch. "Are we ready? I'm just dying to see her face when she opens that door and sees us standing there!"

"She'll open her eyes wide," said Kim reminiscently, "in the way she does when she's taken aback over something; then she'll beam all over her face, and fling her arms around the three of us –" Kim broke off, giving a small deprecating laugh. "You can see the picture as well as I. We all know Mumsie like the backs of our hands."

"Indeed yes," mused Pauline on a tender note. "After the exclamations of surprise and disbelief she'll accept our presents and her eyes will fill up, just a little. Then she'll become all brisk and want to know how we managed to be here, and when we tell her she'll ask whether we really could afford to come or whether we've had to go without things in order to save for the trip. She always did insist on knowing every single detail about everything."

"Because of the motherly interest she had in us all – and still has, for that matter."

"Even though it's three years since the last of us left her most comfortable nest." Pauline frowned slightly as she added, "It was sad in a way that each of us found a job in a different part of the country. It put an end to that lovely time when we were all together."

7

"When we left school, you mean? – and got our first jobs and decided to stay with Mumsie as boarders?"

"That's right. But she insisted on our looking about and bettering ourselves, even though she knew it would be a wrench if we left her. However, we did leave, one by one. Kim was the last to go. I remember Mumsie saying she'd throw her out if she hung on much longer."

Kim nodded, recalling how she had at her foster-mother's insistence applied for an excellent post that was advertised and, having obtained it, decided not to take it, but to stay on at home.

"I'm keeping to my present job," Kim had said, but her foster-mother had become angry, saying she was not having anyone sacrificing her future for her, or being tied to her apron strings. She hadn't brought up the girls with anything like that in mind. Her job was done and now each was free to make her own future in the way that suited her best.

"We all owe a great deal to Mumsie," said Kim at last, and the others inclined their heads in agreement. "She's been both mother and father to us, and if ever I have an opportunity of repaying her I shall not hesitate, no matter what the cost or trouble – or even risk."

"Hear, hear!" from the others in unison. "And we'd be with you, Kim, all the way," added Pauline, little knowing just how soon she was to remember that promise.

Enid was becoming impatient; she frowned at Kim, indicating that she should get on with the tying up of her parcel.

"I'm ready, Enid," she smiled, taking up the parcel after fastening a rosette over the knot in the ribbon with which the parcel was tied. "Where's my bag – Thanks, Pauline. All right? Are we off?"

Half an hour later, having alighted from the bus, they were standing on the step of the pretty blue and white villa, looking round at the flowers and the tall palm trees growing in the garden.

"Isn't it sweet?" from Enid in a quiet voice. "Just exactly as it looked on the snaps Mumsie sent us –"

"Hush – here comes someone!" Pauline held up a finger for silence. All three were tensed, a little breathless from excitement and anticipation. To be in a position to give pleasure was surely the most wonderful thing in the world, decided Kim, automatically patting a stray lock of hair into place. Mumsie had loved the colour of her hair from the moment of setting eyes on her, recalled Kim with a smile. Auburn, Mrs. Rowe had said, gazing down at it, then touching one of the pigtails with a caressing hand. Auburn, with darker shades of russet-brown just to add a little more beauty and charm.

The door opened and swung inwards. Mrs. Marcoras, as she now was, opened her eyes wide, as Kim had predicted ... but they were red-rimmed and swollen, and the smiles instantly froze on the girls' lips.

"Children ... my loves!" Bewilderment could not cover the sob that caught at the words, and the girls glanced uneasily at one another. "Where have you come from? How have you got here? It's an answer to a prayer!"

"A prayer?" echoed Enid anxiously. "Something's wrong?"

"Very wrong." Mrs. Marcoras caught her lip between her teeth to stop its trembling. "But come in, my loves. My, what am I keeping you standing there for?" The three entered a bright arcaded hall, furnished in the modern style and with flowers growing from pots and climbing up the walls. Turning, Kim said, her keen gaze on her foster-mother's tear-stained face,

"Diana . . . she's ill, or something?"

"Not ill – It were better if she were! Oh, that you should all come, at this particular moment, when I had said to myself, 'If only the girls were here they'd think of something – especially Kim, who always had such good ideas when it came to troubles.' You had the most unorthodox notions, but they always worked, if you remember? Yes, they always worked . . . although I can't see what you can think up on this occasion –"

"Darling," cut in Kim gently, "you haven't told us what's wrong with Diana." She glanced at Pauline, then at Enid. Diana was a nice girl, on the whole, but she did have a most obstinate streak that had caused her mother a good deal of anxiety in the past. "She's in some trouble, obviously?"

Dumbly Mrs. Marcoras nodded, but then she brushed her anxiety aside for the moment as she took in the parcels the girls carried, and the flowers. Tears filled her eyes as she spoke.

"You've come, on my birthday. Th-thank y-you. . . ."

The three girls looked at one another, deflated, and feeling their presents were totally out of place. "Thank you," said Mrs. Marcoras again, trying to adopt a cheerful manner but failing miserably. "Come into the living-room. Petros is at the office – but I expect you'll have guessed that."

Kim was frowning heavily. She knew her foster-mother was weighed down with anxiety and grief.

"Tell us what's wrong, Mumsie darling," she pressed. "We want to know at once."

10

"But you –" Her lip quivered and a sob escaped her. "You all looked so excited and expectant when I opened the door. You've come today, though I still don't know how you've managed it –"

"We took our holidays so that we could be with you," interrupted Pauline, feeling some small explanation would not detract too much from the more important issues. "We promised, if you remember?"

"Indeed I remember, but never did I expect you'd be able to keep your promise, not with my being here, in Athens."

"We thought you wouldn't, and that's why we were so excited . . ." Enid's voice trailed away and she bit her lip in vexation at the impulse that had brought forth those words. Mrs. Marcoras looked at the parcel she held under her arm and burst into tears.

"You planned it all, and bought me presents, and all I've done is to spoil your pleasure. Why did it have to happen now?" she cried, taking the flowers from Pauline and holding them to her face. The girls glanced at one another unhappily, thinking how different this was from what they had so eagerly anticipated. "Come into the living-room," she invited again, and led the way into a pretty apartment which had a view on to the front garden.

"Now," said Kim briskly when they were all seated, "we'll have your news."

"Diana's got herself mixed up with a married man of over forty years of age," began Mrs. Marcoras without further hesitation. "He's a Greek, has two children by his second wife and four by a previous one." She lowered her head and stared at the flowers which she held on her knee. A swift glance passed between Enid and Pauline, but Kim was grimly regarding her foster mother's bent head.

"You mean," she inquired presently, "that she and he are having an affair?"

"That's what I mean, Kim," came the choked whisper, and Kim felt a lump rise in her throat. Mumsie had been such a stickler for clean living. There was nothing to be gained, she used to drill into the girls as they grew into their teens, by having lovers before marriage. That idea was out of date now, but Kim had no need to stretch her imagination to realize what her foster-mother was suffering.

"How do you know this? Surely Diana hasn't told you?"

"No, she never mentioned the man until I did. I learned of the affair from a sister of the man's wife. She came here and told me that they were going about together, and that his wife was broken-hearted over it. She asked me to intervene, to stop my daughter from seeing him." Mrs. Marcoras lifted her face; Kim flinched at its expression. That she should have had to suffer the humiliation of having someone come to her door and inform her that her seventeen-year-old daughter was having an affair with a married man ... Kim's temper rose; it showed in that light in those green eyes; it showed in the colour tinting her cheeks, in the sudden compression of her mouth, a mouth which was normally full and generous, and that could be compassionate when the need for compassion arose. The other two girls exchanged glances. Was Kim on the verge of one of her very rare furies? they wondered.

"You tackled Diana, obviously?"

"At once! She seemed sorry for hurting me, but refused to give him up –"

"Didn't you point out how profitless such an association was?" interrupted Pauline, frowning darkly

12

from her chair at the other side of the room.

"She wouldn't listen to anything I had to say, Pauline. She's infatuated with the man, and flattered, I expect, as these young girls are when a man of that age becomes interested in them."

"Wasn't she ashamed?" asked Enid, and Mrs. Marcoras instantly shook her head.

"Not in the least. I couldn't believe I was speaking to my own daughter, so brazenly did she answer me. He was a fine man, misunderstood by his wife," she said.

"Not that tale!" flashed Kim derisively. "It's been going since Adam! Men!" she said grittingly. "Why do they always fall back on that lame excuse? Can't they face up to the fact that they themselves have failings?" She stood up and a formidable figure she appeared, her eyes glinting like polished malachite, her teeth pressed tightly together, her fists clenched. Her temper was fast rising, though inwardly, since there was no one here against whom it could be directed. Usually she was cool and calm, but she had always been the strong one, the forceful one, the prop on which Mumsie would lean on the rare occasions when support was needed.

"You haven't told us everything," she said at last, watching her foster-mother's face closely.

"No, not by any means." The words came to a faltering stop and tears swiftly gathered in Mumsie's eyes. "You remember when I opened the door to you just now that I remarked on your arriving at that particular moment?" Kim nodded, and she continued, in halting accents edged with despair, "I had just found a letter – in the pocket of one of Diana's dresses which I was about to wash. It was written by her to the man Takis, and as several alterations had been made I

13

guessed it was a rough draft and she had forgotten to destroy it. The corrected version will of course have been posted –" Again she stopped, and Kim swallowed a lump in her throat as she watched the tears fall on to Mumsie's pale cheeks. "Diana's agreed to go away with him," she managed at last, searching for a handkerchief with which to dry her eyes. "They're going on Tuesday evening."

"Diana's agreed to run off with him – a man old enough to be her father?" interrupted Enid, staring in disbelief. "Is she intending to spend the rest of her life with him?"

"Your husband," said Kim practically before Mrs. Marcoras could reply to Enid's question. "Can't he do anything to prevent this?"

"He's entirely ignorant of the affair, Kim. I haven't dared tell him, for in Greece this sort of behaviour on the part of a young girl is considered to be scandalous in the extreme. Petros would be horrified were he to learn that his stepdaughter of seventeen, whom he would expect to be chaste, was having an affair with a married man – or any man, for that matter. It would so shock him that it must inevitably affect our marriage, happy though we are."

"He couldn't attach any blame to you," said Kim indignantly."

"No, but it would affect him deeply. He would think of the scandal, and of his friends and business associates knowing of the affair."

"Can we see this letter?" asked Kim at length. Already her brain was working furiously, but as yet she saw no way of preventing the elopement. "If you don't want us to see it then don't be afraid of saying so."

"I want you to see it." Rising, Mumsie looked into

14

Kim's stern set face. "Have – have you thought of anything – of any way of stopping them?"

"Not yet."

"But you will?" eagerly and more than a little confidently.

"I'll try – but, darling, please don't begin hoping yet, for I haven't even the germ of one of those unorthodox notions you mentioned just now."

Mrs. Marcoras nodded and went out, returning a moment or two later with the letter, which she passed to Kim. The other two girls rose and read over her shoulders.

"Well," said Pauline when at length they had all taken in what the letter contained, "Diana seems quite determined to go with the man."

"How could she do this to you!" exclaimed Enid wrathfully. "I can't think what's come over her!"

"She was always wilful, you know that. I have to admit it, even though she's my own daughter."

"One thing stands out," murmured Kim almost to herself. "She says here that, if he lets her down, she'll never speak to him again. This would seem to mean that she isn't entirely sure of him?"

"It's funny you should say that. I gained the same impression, but not only from the letter. When I tackled her about this man, she was obstinate and determined not to give him up, but all the time she seemed troubled, and although I couldn't have found a reason for it I felt, somehow, that she wasn't quite sure of him."

Kim perused the first paragraph again.

"I'll come away with you, Takis darling. There never was any doubt in my mind, but as I told you, I had to give it more thought. I love Mum and hate the idea of hurting her, but mums get over these things,

15

and in any case, I love you ten – no, twenty times more than I love her. We'll live in this house you've bought in Sparta, and no one will ever know we're not married. I'll be at the Imperial at seven o'clock on Tuesday evening and you'll be in the black Mercedes, you said? I know you'll be there before me, having a few drinks in the hotel, so please leave the car unlocked so that I can get in and wait for you. Park at the end, right under the trees, won't you? Then no one will see me get into the car. I know you think I'm silly, but all those lights at the front of the hotel daunt me – they always have when we've been there, dining and dancing – for we seem to be the object of everyone's prying eyes. Inside, the lights are so subtly shaded, aren't they? – and so I never feel conspicuous. Be there, Takis, because if you let me down I shall never speak to you again."

Slowly Kim folded the letter, having no desire to re-read the rest, which was, to her mind, nothing but slop, revealing the lovesick mind of the writer.

"Of course," she murmured thoughtfully, "you can't be sure she has sent a letter to this Takis, can you?"

"She's going away with him, Kim. All her clothes have been to the dry-cleaners; she's bought a whole pile of undies and frilly nightgowns and the rest. They're hidden away in a box under her bed. I found it," ended Mumsie, blushing.

"What a damnable situation!" Pauline scowled as she sat down again. "The man wants beating up, or kidnapping, or something," she ended vaguely.

Silence, as Kim turned slowly and faced her friend.

"What did you say?" she murmured at length.

"He ought to be punished in some way that would prevent his carrying out this elopement. Oh, if only we were men!"

Kim continued to stare at her, the germ of an idea already conceived, emerging from some obscure recess of her mind from where at odd times in the past had come those other unorthodox notions of which Mumsie had spoken.

"And what," inquired Kim softly of her friend, "could we do if we were men?"

"Well," began Pauline rather uncertainly, "we could – er – use our strength on the fellow – not beat him up exactly, but threaten him, or give him a good punch on the nose if need be."

"Or kidnap him," said Kim, but to herself. If the man could be prevented from being at the rendezvous at the appointed time then Diana must inevitably accept that she had been let down. And if she meant what she said – and somehow Kim felt sure she did – then she would never speak to the man again. True, he would eventually tell her he'd been kidnapped, but surely any girl with an ounce of nous would laugh such an explanation to scorn.

"It's by no means perfect," she was later to admit to her friends, "but in the absence of any other plan we really must give it a trial." Meanwhile, though, she and the others remained with their foster-mother until midnight. They met Petros and liked him enormously, and he in turn appeared to be most favourably impressed with them. They chatted to Diana when she arrived home from the office with her stepfather, acting as if they were in ignorance of her affair with the Greek. She remained in during the evening, so it seemed that she and Takis were not to meet until the evening of the departure for Sparta, in her lover's black Mercedes. Not many of those about, Kim had mused on reading this. People these days usually preferred something brighter than black.

At last the good nights were said and the girls were at the front door of the villa, saying a last few words to Mumsie.

"I know you've thought of something," she had said earlier, "for I can tell by your expression." However, she had refrained from asking questions, knowing Kim so well as she did. Kim never spoke of any plan she had made until it was well developed from the embryo stage. However, she now put a tentative question, which Kim answered in a grim determined voice.

"I certainly have a plan in mind, and I feel it can be made to work. Briefly, I'm planning to keep the fellow away from the meeting-place, so that it will appear that he's let Diana down. If my plan's successful then we just have to keep our fingers crossed that Diana means what she says, and that she'll be finished with him forever – No, darling, no more questions. And although we'd love to be with you tomorrow, and every day while we're here, on holiday, it isn't possible as things have turned out. The preparations for the scheme are complicated, to put it mildly, and we haven't much time, as you already know."

"Bless you! But I knew you'd think up something. Loves –" she looked at the others in turn, "you knew she had something brewing, didn't you?"

They nodded.

"I'm just dying to know what it is," said Pauline. But when she did know what it was she at first expressed doubts about being able to carry out the plan successfully. Enid was also doubtful, and Kim herself agreed that it was not going to be easy to abduct a grown man, one who, according to Mumsie, was well above average height, and athletically built as well.

18

But as always, Kim had a firm trust in herself, and after all, there were three of them, she told her friends.

"Three to one," she was repeating a couple of nights later as she and the others sat in a corner of the hotel lounge, going over details of Kim's plan, "and none of us can remotely be described as a weakling. I myself might look fragile, but I'm jolly well not!"

"Can I buy you both a drink?" asked Pauline as the waiter approached from the other side of the lounge. "Enid, your usual?"

"Lovely, thanks."

"Not at the moment, thanks, Pauline. I need a clear head for this business." Kim had an open notebook on the table in front of her and now and then she would jot something down. "The most difficult part is getting a man's voice on to your tape recorder, Enid," she said when, having received the order, the waiter moved out of earshot. "How the dickens are we to make some man say, 'Drive on, and don't turn your head' or some such thing? — I haven't worked out all the words yet because I've not quite got the route from the Imperial to that cottage we've rented. We must be up at the crack of dawn tomorrow and hire a taxi to take us there, by the shortest route."

"Is it safe to get a taxi?"

"Of course. We'll not have one come here for us, though. We'll get one in Omonia Square, from where thousands of people hire them."

"You know," Pauline was saying as she watched the waiter coming towards them with his tray a few minutes later, "I don't expect these fellows are at all well paid in these hotels."

Kim frowned at her.

"Do keep to the point, Pauline. We need three

19

heads, all the time."

"Very gullible, these lower classes of Greeks," mused Pauline, as if Kim's words had not even registered, "yes, very gullible. They'll believe anything. And if there's a quid going into the bloke's palm . . ." She tailed off as the man came closer. A row of even white teeth were revealed in a smile as he put down their drinks on the table.

"Thank you, madam –" He broke off, staring at the tip. "Thank you very much! *Efharisto poli.*"

"What's going on?" Enid wanted to know, ignoring her drink. "Since when have you been able to afford a tip like that?"

"You've an idea," murmured Kim softly. "Out with it, Pauline."

"If we tell that fellow that we're amateur actresses from England, and that when we go back we're putting on a play with a Greek setting, and we need a voice with a Greek accent, a voice that will come from backstage – Need I go on?" she asked in a tone which was a mingling of triumph and pride.

"Pauline, I take my hat off to you!" Kim's face cleared miraculously. "I'll have that drink now – and enjoy it!"

CHAPTER TWO

WITH all the plans made and checked, and every step of the operation having been rehearsed, the three girls sat in Kim's bedroom and went over the whole procedure for the last time before it was actually to be carried out.

"I can't foresee any real snags," declared Kim with

20

confidence. She glanced up suddenly. "You're quite sure Mumsie's got the correct message to give to Diana? I'd hate a small thing like a message to upset all our plans. Mumsie does get muddled at times. What exactly is she going to say to Diana? Did you get her to repeat it to you when you rang?"

"Yes, and I wrote it down as she did so. I'll get the paper." Rising, Pauline went to the door connecting her room with Kim's. The message was in shorthand and Kim read,

"A man came on the phone this afternoon and asked me to give you a message. He didn't give his name, but I expect you know who it is. He said to tell you he can't possibly make it for seven owing to a last-minute business engagement, so it will have to be eight. He said you mustn't try to contact him on any account. I thought it was a very vague sort of message and I told him so. I then asked him to give me a clearer explanation, but he wouldn't. He said you would know what he meant. Eight, not seven. I suppose it's a dinner date or something with that dreadful man. I do wish you'd give him up, Diana."

Kim smiled a tender smile, and a satisfied one.

"Practically the very words I gave her myself over the phone. Did she ask any questions?"

"She started to," grinned Pauline. "But I said I was in the heck of a hurry and put down the receiver. Poor darling!"

"And now," said Kim briskly, "just once more. We begin by driving our hired car into the grounds of the Imperial Hotel at six-thirty. . . ."

"We'll park here, where it's quiet, yet not anywhere near where we expect Takis to park." Kim edged the car between two others and switched off the engine.

"I wonder if he's arrived yet?" The three girls got out of the car, collected what was required, and then closed and locked the doors. "I feel strangely devoid of any sensation," murmured Kim, her glance having caught the huge black car parked not very far from where they were standing. "Is that it?" she frowned. "We'd decided Takis would park under those trees – that's where Diana told him to park."

"That's it all right," from Pauline, whose voice seemed to tremble a little. "A black Mercedes. Obviously Takis wasn't pandering to Diana's wish for complete privacy."

"I wonder why?" Kim was walking towards the car, her friends following closely. She was dressed in black trews and sweater; the others wore their ordinary clothes. Yesterday they had viewed the place where they expected Takis to park, and had felt elated at the seclusion afforded by the clump of giant oak trees that formed a miniature area of woodland at the extreme end of the hotel grounds. It seemed an ideal place for the runaways to meet, and yet Takis had parked here. However, there were no lights anywhere close and on peering into the back of the car Kim said it would be quite all right; she would never be seen.

There followed three or four busy minutes, with Kim getting into the car and finding the most comfortable position, as there was almost half an hour to wait. The other two covered her with a black rug, tucking it around her. She had a black beret on her head, her auburn hair tucked up into it. In one hand she clutched a small tape recorder, in the other a short piece of wood.

"Are you all right?" whispered Enid, clearly troubled now that the actual plan was being put into operation. "You're not scared?"

"Scared?" laughed Kim. "I've never been scared in my life!"

"Supposing he does happen to see this lump down here?"

"Then he'll yank me out – and I shall run as fast as my legs will carry me – But don't let's contemplate failure, Enid. This has got to work, for Mumsie's sake!"

"Had we better stay around until he comes?" began Pauline anxiously. "We can sit in the car."

"No, that wouldn't do at all. You've to be at the cottage when we arrive. You'd better get moving at once, just in case you lose your way or something."

"Yes. It is an out-of-the-way place. The man could die there if we left him, for I'm sure no one ever goes to that lonely spot." Pauline banged the door on her side of the car. From the other side Enid said, "Watch *you* don't lose your way. You don't want to be in here with that rogue a moment longer than is necessary."

"I'll take care," promised Kim. "I've the entire route mapped out in my mind. I'll not get lost."

"So long, then – and good luck!" The door closed and an eerie silence settled on the car. Straining her ears, Kim heard the hired car start up, then the sound of the engine dying away. She lay still, relaxing her muscles but not her mind, as she went over what would take place once Takis was behind the wheel of his car. He would be forced to drive to the lonely cottage they had rented – rented for a week as the house agent would not let them have it for less time than that. Once at the cottage he would be locked up in the room they had prepared for him. No locks were on the door of the room originally, so the girls had fixed two large bolts on the outside, one at the top and one at the bottom. Food had already been put in, and water. He would be kept a prisoner for at least twenty-four hours, although Enid wanted him to be left to cool his courage for longer than that.

"Might as well leave him there until we're ready to go home, which is five days from now," Enid had said as they were setting out from their hotel just over an hour ago. "We could go each day and give him his ration of bread and water."

"Really, Enid, you're even more barbaric than I," Kim had laughed, but she also had secretly thought that a longer period of confinement would have done the rogue a deal of good.

Her thoughts were brought to an abrupt halt as the car door opened and she found herself holding her breath. It was a matter of seconds before the man was at the wheel; Kim's nostrils were filled with a most pleasant smell. After-shave lotion? But no, it could not possibly be. Takis wasn't staying at the hotel. She still held her breath, for not a sound could be heard from the man in front. What was he doing? Was he surprised that Diana had not yet turned up? She had said she would be waiting in the car. . . .

With a little silent gasp Kim heard the engine catch and within seconds the car was moving. Where was the man going already? He hadn't waited more than a couple of minutes for Diana – and in any case, Kim felt sure it was not yet seven o'clock. The car was almost out on the road before she began to move, so great was her surprise. However, she soon collected herself and, quietly easing herself up until she could sit on the edge of the seat, she placed the tape recorder on her knee, making sure she kept out of the line of the driving-mirror. The piece of wood was pushed between the man's shoulder blades and the recorder

24

switched on, the microphone switch being used, as it made no sound.

"Don't speak or turn your head," said the accentated voice from the recorder. "Follow the instructions I shall give you. If you speak you won't be answered. Our journey isn't long – about half an hour." The man gave one small quiver of surprise, or was it apprehension? Kim was unable to guess which. Takis would be a coward, she and her friends had agreed, but somehow Kim gained the impression that he was far from being afraid. "Turn right here and carry on for about a mile. Turn left at the crossroads."

All went with almost unbelievable smoothness, and as the great car turned into the narrow lane leading to the cottage she saw the light streaming forth from one of the windows.

"We're clever," she whispered exultantly to herself as, having been given the order, Takis was bringing the car to a standstill half-way along the lane. From here on it was no more than a track three or four feet wide. "What a fool he's going to feel when he sees the tape recorder and my little wooden peg! "

"Keep going! " the recorder snapped out when they had both left the car, "and don't dare to turn your head. You're covered from the cottage as well! " No sound from the man. Although he had been ordered not to speak it did seem strange that, even now when he was almost at his destination, he asked no questions at all.

They were walking along the track; the girls would be waiting, one either side of the door, ready to bring him down if he should suddenly decide to put up a fight. Kim's heart began to beat a little faster now for this was the part that could not be rehearsed. She

25

hoped the man would go meekly into the room that had been prepared for him and, once he was safely secured, they could all relax. If however he should decide to put up some resistance he would have to be tackled, by the three of them, and Kim could only hope and pray that they would be just that little bit more than a match for him that they could bundle him into the room and lock him in.

The man's steps seemed to be slowing down and Kim gave him a jab with the wood. Again he quivered; she sensed it rather than saw it . . . and she also sensed that he was in a fury. Of course, this was only natural, she thought, her eyes on the tiny pool just ahead, to the right of the track. Its rim came to the edge of the track, and just behind it grew a huge chestnut tree. The man's steps *were* becoming slower. . . . And at the pool was a bend in the lane which would shut out the cottage lights for a moment. There were no more instructions on the tape recorder and as she herself could not give any Kim just kept on prodding at the man's back. How difficult it was to remember not to speak! Kim had never before realized this. She was just dying to order Takis to get a move on! They came level with the pool and Kim held her breath, for the stench was vile. Some noxious water-weed must have gone bad, she thought, wondering why someone didn't come along and clean it out. It must be breeding mosquitoes. How dark it was, now that the bend was reached and the cottage lights had disappeared. Some urgency caused her to give the man's back a vicious jab, for he really was slowing down –

Her thoughts were cut as the blow landed on her face; she felt herself go staggering back, right across the tiny pool, felt the excruciating impact as her head hit the tree; she saw stars reflected on the pond, and

26

then blackness descended upon her. . . .

"Oh, my head!" Kim opened her eyes and allowed her glazed vision to take in the white walls, and the porthole. Where was she? She put a hand to the back of her head; the lump felt as big as a football. "What happened?" Someone opened the door and a man stood there, a tall man and slender, but strong-looking . . . three men . . . no, two. . . . She began to rub her eyes, then cried out in pain. "Who are you?" She brought him properly into focus. Yes, only one. . . .

"The man who gave you the black eye."

"The –?" It was all coming back now. Kim gingerly touched her left eye. Was it closed? She covered the other eye and found she could not see a thing. Her cheek was puffed up and the side of her mouth also appeared to be affected, for her lip felt swollen. That blow must have come up from her mouth to her eye, and to her temple. "Takis. . . ." She stared at him with her good eye. Over forty? This man was no more than thirty, even though he had a few sprinklings of grey at his temples. "You're Takis?" She felt her senses leaving her again and in an effort to prevent this she struggled to a sitting position. "What –!" Blushing hotly, she slid down, bringing up the covers right to her chin. "Where am I?"

"In bed." There was a distinct hint of amusement in his voice, but there was a grim note too, and his narrowed eyes were glinting at her in the most disturbing way.

"Would you mind telling me exactly what happened?" Even in this, the most vulnerable position possible, Kim managed somehow to inject a note of hauteur into her voice. "Obviously the tables have been turned –"

"Well and truly turned!" Suddenly he looked different; the hint of humour vanished and she saw before her a man with an ugly twist to his mouth and a gleam of sheer evil in his eyes – and such dark eyes they were! Black, almost, and piercing below straight brows – haughty brows yet noble too, like his features, despite their formidable lines. Yes, they were noble, and so very, very Greek. "You, a female, daring to threaten me! – to prod and poke and thrust a gun in my back! By God, girl, you're going to pay dear for it! Yes, the tables are turned, and had you known me better you'd have watched your step more carefully. No one – man or woman – prods me in the back and gets away with it. I'll have you screaming out for mercy over and over again before I've finished with you! – third-rate little crook that you are!"

Kim's heart had given a great lurch as he began to speak and now it thudded against her ribs. She had never been afraid in her life, she had recently boasted. . . .

"You were intent on ruining someone I know," she began, then faltered to a stop. Her brain was by no means clear, but she was acutely aware of something seriously amiss. Strange prickles started at the base of her neck and ran down the whole length of her spine. This man was surely not the father of six children, nor – as she had already decided – was he anywhere near forty years of age. His air of superiority, too, did not seem to fit in with the picture she had formed of Diana's lover. "Are – are you Takis?" she asked.

"Takis who?" and without waiting for an answer, "The name's Souris – Damon Souris – but you know what my name is! You and your accomplices learned all about me before you planned the abduction –" He broke off; the very word, when associated with himself, seemed to add tinder to his smouldering wrath. "Yes, you learned all about me. I'm not the first businessman to be snatched by thugs!"

"Snatched by thugs?" What a nasty-sounding expression.... Kim blinked with her good eye, for everything was beginning to dart about, out of focus. Her head was throbbing with a sickening pain ... and now she was drifting away somewhere.... "No, it isn't anything to do with thugs. It was Takis we wanted ... he was running off with Diana ... no, Mr. Souris, it wasn't you we wanted at all.... I'm very sorry for the inconvenience...." She mustn't become unconscious again, decided Kim, fiercely endeavouring to hold on to her senses, dulled though they were. This man looked dangerous and something disastrous could happen to her if she was not careful. Lifting her head from the pillow, she moved it from side to side hoping this would clear it a little, but sword points shot through it and she groaned in agony. "My head," she said again, looking appealingly at the man by the door. His dark face was a severe unsmiling mask, the expression in his eyes one of deep contempt. "I'm in great pain," she faltered as it grew even worse. "I can't *think*."

"The pain will go with time," he said heartlessly, and would have left her, but she cried out as he turned,

"You must listen to me! I'm innocent—"

"Innocent?" he echoed in incredulous tones. And then, faintly shrugging his shoulders, "Your senses are impaired, naturally—"

"They are, but they're becoming clearer now. Please stay, Mr. Souris, and allow me to explain." She paused a moment and once more looked appealingly at him, quite unaware of the fact that her face was so deformed by the blow he had given her that

29

she looked positively ugly. Her mouth and cheek were swollen, her eye black and blue and closed by the puffiness around it. Above it was an angry cut, with the blood clotted over it. "If I'm not too clear then please be patient, because my mind keeps becoming blurred, sort of. But I shall be speaking nothing but the truth." He drew an exasperated breath which made her continue urgently, thankful that her bout of dizziness was passing and that she was able to collect her thoughts into some sort of order. "This Takis I spoke of was having an affair with my foster-mother's daughter, and they were intending to run away together. He was married and had six children –" She stopped on noting the sudden twist of sardonic humour that had replaced the evil aspect of his mouth.

"Six?" he repeated. "I wonder why it's always six?" He spoke with the trace of an accent, which registered with Kim in spite of the state she was in. And she even had time to think that it was most attractive before she said,

"He really did have six – well, that's what Mumsie heard. Mumsie's my foster-mother," she explained, feeling the necessity for an explanation, as his brows had lifted faintly. She continued with her story, faltering now and then as darts of sheer torture shot through her head. On reaching the end of her narrative she found her hopes sinking into her feet. This Damon Souris not only disbelieved her, he also despised her for even thinking up such an unconvincing story. She saw this in his expression even before he spoke.

"What a deplorably weak attempt to extricate yourself," he sneered, his eyes flicking her face with acute disdain. "Even in your present state you surely could have thought up something more convincing than that.

Not that it would have worked. Nothing you can say will help you; you're in for a bad time when this trip's over and I get you to my home."

Her heart gave a sickening lurch, much more painfully this time than before.

"Where am I?" she faltered. The porthole, which had scarcely registered on her first noticing it, so dazed was her mind, took on a deep significance now. "This trip you mention . . .?"

"You're aboard my yacht. And we're on our way to the island of Cos, where I live."

"Cos?" she repeated dazedly. "But what object can you have for taking me there?" Her mind was failing again, dulled by pain. If only she could keep a clear head! she thought desperately, she might even yet be able to convince this man that it was not him they had planned to kidnap, and if she *could* convince him then he would surely turn round and take her back to Piraeus, for that was obviously the port from which they had sailed.

"You're going to pay for daring to threaten me – I've already told you that. At first I did think of letting the police deal with you, but then it would all have come out and I'd no intention of suffering the indignity of admitting I was held up by a woman –" He stopped and the most ugly light entered his eyes. Kim wondered if he would ever recover from the humiliation he had experienced at her hands. "As I was not allowing you to go free I decided to give you a dose of your own medicine. You yourself are being abducted –"

"You must listen to me!" she broke in desperately as thoughts flashed one after another through her mind, mingling her own danger with so many other aspects of this dire situation in which she had landed

31

herself. "My foster-mother will be frantic, and so will my two friends who were at the cottage –"

"Your confederates, you mean? I expect they'll have fled, and forgotten all about you."

"We were on holiday together, as I told you – Oh, *please*, Mr. Souris, just listen – and be prepared to believe what you hear. I know how you feel, and that you must be furiously angry at what happened to you. I can only apologize, and ask you to be very understanding and – and forgiving." Kim stopped abruptly, silenced by the spurning flick of his hand.

"I'm listening to nothing. I know exactly what you and your dirty little band of amateur crooks were up to. You've read the papers, focused your greedy eyes on those fantastic sums that have recently been paid for the return of kidnapped businessmen, and you thought you might as well cash in." His fine lips curled in a sneer of contempt. "You despicable rat! I've heard of your Women's Rights, or Lib, or whatever name you have for such nonsense, but I didn't know you'd progressed as far as to enter the crime business in order to emulate your men."

Kim listened, understandingly and yet indignantly as he proceeded to flick her with his scorn. His pride had received a crushing blow and were she in his place she too would have been in a mood of fury. But on the other hand, she felt she would at least have pondered over the explanation given, and acquired more information by putting questions of her own. Men, though, she thought impatiently, were always too quick in their judgements! They condemned without a hearing and that was why they made so many stupid mistakes. This man was going to feel more than a little ridiculous on learning of his mistake, as sooner or later he must learn of it.

But so much could happen before that time, for there was something almost fiendish in the expression of this dark Greek standing there, arms folded, his attitude that of a judge.

"I'm not a criminal, Mr. Souris," she persisted, then allowed her voice to trail away to silence. She was in such great pain, from the swelling on the back of her head and from her face and eye, that to persevere was too much of an effort. Besides, there were other things of importance troubling her, one of which was the discovery that she was stark naked beneath these bedclothes . . . and she wondered how she came to be stripped . . . and by whom?

"My clothes," she said, turning her head to hide her blushes. "Did you –? I mean, where are they?"

"I did. And they're in the bath. You can wash them if you're feeling up to it."

"I feel awful. Did you know, when you hit me, that I was a woman?"

"No, I didn't." The evil expression was relaxed for the moment and he appeared much more human, though there was still an austerity about his finely-chiselled features which she suspected was a permanent part of his make-up. "Your tape recorder was a brilliant idea, but proves that clever as you and your accomplices were a man was necessary for the working of your plan. It's here –" He flicked a finger towards a small table on which the recorder lay. "The gun went into the pool, along with you. I couldn't at first make up my mind whether to fish you out or turn you over on to your face and let you smother in the mud. However, when I felt to see if your heart was still beating I decided to bring you out –" He broke off, actually laughing as the colour flooded into her face. That laugh transformed his features in the most dramatic way and, diverted for a second, Kim stared at him, fascinated. There was something strangely contradictory about the man, she decided. Perhaps his was a dual personality . . . and if so, then she could still hope. "Blushing! Well, well, women are the most unpredictable creatures! A hardened little would-be crook – the moll of some petty thug, I shouldn't wonder – and yet she can blush."

"I'm not the moll of some petty thug!" she flashed, then immediately groaned in pain. Her face twisted. "My head . . . can't you do something for me?" It was a cry from the heart; she forgot everything except her agony as she added, "Give me a tablet, please."

"Do something for you?" The straight dark brows lifted a fraction. "After that gun-play –?"

"I didn't have a gun."

His eyes opened wide.

"No? Then what, might I ask, was repeatedly prodded –" He broke off and she heard his teeth snap together and saw the tightening of his mouth and the dark streak of colour crept slowly up the sides of it. "What was repeatedly prodded into my back?"

She hesitated, realizing just how absurd the truth would sound. Besides, she knew for sure that such was this man's pride that he would far rather it were a gun that had forced him to obedience than a small piece of wood no more lethal than a clothes peg.

"Never mind," she said at last. "It isn't important."

He glanced oddly at her but made no effort to pursue the matter. And as he was still in the more human mood Kim made even yet another attempt to get the truth through to him. But she had only just begun when her voice faded. "He's gone! Why won't he listen? Oh, my pains! I need medical attention!" she shouted in anger and frustration. "Perhaps I do sound

34

insincere, but I can't think properly, and neither would you if you felt the way I do ! Listen to me, I tell you! Listen!" No sound from beyond the open doorway and, managing to separate the sheet from the blanket, she wrapped herself in it. But it slipped as she got off the bed and Damon Souris chose that moment to return, a small bottle in his hand. Frantically she grabbed the sheet, aware of the expression of sardonic amusement written on his dark and arrogant face. "Can I have a drink of water?" she asked in a small voice, not noticing the bottle he held, for her senses were swiftly becoming dulled again. This inability to think was a blessing in a way, since the situation appeared much less fraught with danger, and the man who was responsible for it much less formidable. She was red in the face still, resulting from her embarrassment of a few seconds ago, and as she glanced up she saw that he was still considerably amused. The dark eyes seemed alive with – she fervently hoped! – humour. "My throat feels like sandpaper."

"It will do," he returned heartlessly, "from the sand and grit and other filth you must have swallowed on falling into that pool."

A great shudder passed through Kim's slender body.

"The water?" she begged. Thoughts were mere snatches of memory now; they darted about in her mind. Mumsie optimistically believing the girls were pulling off some miracle ... the two girls themselves wondering what could have happened to her. They'd go to the police, merely reporting her missing, for they dared not mention the plot to abduct Takis. Mumsie would then have to be told ... poor darling, as if she hadn't enough to think about. What had transpired regarding the elopement? Kim wondered, then impatiently dismissed the matter. She had more important things to worry her now. The police . . . they'd begin a search, but how could they possibly find her, here on the yacht of Damon Souris, a man of whom Enid and Pauline had never even heard and, consequently, they would be unable to give the police a clue. "Mumsie will be broken-hearted," Kim quivered in a hoarse cracked voice. "Mr. Souris, you have no idea the trouble you're causing me."

He was pouring water from a carafe; he handed it to her as he spoke.

"This is nothing to the trouble you intended causing me." He uncorked the bottle. "Here — aspirins. They should ease your pain."

"Thank you," she said gratefully, accepting the two tablets from him. Swallowing them, she drank deeply, until the glass was emptied. As he made no attempt to take the glass she was holding out to him she went over to the pretty little dressing-table which was fixed to the wall of the cabin. Putting the glass down, she glanced in the mirror. "Good God!" she gasped. "Is that me?"

A laugh rang out from behind her.

"Not a very pretty sight, eh? You should have seen yourself when I first brought you on here. You were caked from head to foot in mud as well as looking like a bruiser who had just taken the beating of his life in a boxing ring."

Slowly she turned; her senses seemed to be leaving her altogether now.

"You — washed m-me?" she faltered.

His dark and arrogant brows lifted.

"Washed? I put you on deck and threw a bucket of water over you. I'd not have done that much had it

36

not been for the necessity of letting you have one of my beds."

Kim hastily changed the subject, for even in her dazed state she had no difficulty in imagining the scene. And even in her dazed state she could understand his treating her with so little feeling or respect. After all, to him she was just a cheap little criminal, someone who had plotted, with the help of confederates, to kidnap him and hold him to ransom.

"My clothes ... they're still wet through, I suppose?"

"They wouldn't be lying in the bath if they weren't." He was leaning with a sort of careless grace against the jamb of the door, immaculate in white slacks and sweater. His arms were folded, his eyes moving slowly over the sheet that covered her. She felt naked under that dark scrutiny, naked and inadequate; with her face swollen and her eye closed she knew that she looked like some grotesquely ugly creature who was totally out of place on this luxurious yacht.

"You put them to soak for me?"

"I? Certainly not!"

Kim coloured and said,

"You just dropped them in – and they're all muddy, I suppose?"

"And they reek. If you go in there to wash them then see that you close the door behind you. I don't want the noisome stench pervading the whole vessel."

He sounded quite heartless, but again she found excuses for him.

"If only you would listen," she said, then stopped, gasping at the searing pain that tore mercilessly at the nerves in her head and neck. "I n-need a doctor," she moaned and slid, senseless, to the floor.

CHAPTER THREE

WHEN she came to she was back in bed; a man was in the cabin, putting something on a chair.

"You wake up? I tell my master."

"Who are you?" The pain had cleared for the present, and so had Kim's brain.

"One of the hands." His face was impassive, but Kim could not help wondering what his thoughts were.

"One of the hands? Mr. Souris has a crew?"

"But of course. At present there are only two of us, because this isn't a pleasure trip, you see." His glance moved to the chair. "My master told me to wash and dry your clothes," he said, and left the cabin before she had time to thank him.

Kim's glance moved from the closed door to the chair. He would tell his master, the man said, so it was risky to get out of bed and begin to dress herself. Better to wait a few minutes, much as she wanted to acquire the protection of her clothes.

And she was glad she had waited. Damon Souris appeared almost immediately, a glass of amber-coloured liquid in his hand.

"Sit up," he ordered curtly, "and drink this."

She eyed it suspiciously.

"What is it?" she began, but was instantly interrupted with,

"I told you to sit up."

Kim fidgeted with the sheet.

"If you would leave it there, on the dressing-table –?"

"Sit up, and don't be so damned coy! It hardly goes

with your personality, and in any case it's a little late for modesty, don't you think? I've seen just about all there is to see – more than once."

"Oh . . ." she quivered, in full possession of her senses now and, mercifully, out of pain. "You're detestable! No man with an atom of delicacy or consideration would remind me of that!"

Damon Souris merely gave a short laugh.

"The air of injured innocence is also superfluous. You're a cheap and rotten little crook, and acting isn't going to get you anywhere. Sit up before I decide to give you some assistance!"

She obeyed even as the half-threat left his lips. The sheet was held in front of her and his eyes kindled with a sort of contemptuous humour.

"It tastes like poison," she shuddered as she gulped down her first taste of the liquid.

"Had I wanted to murder you I'd have stuck my toe under you as you lay in that pond, and turned you over. Drink the rest; it's for your nerves."

"There's nothing wrong with my nerves!" she flashed, becoming more herself with each minute that passed.

"There could be," he warned, grave suddenly and, she thought, just a trifle anxious. "If I'm not mistaken you're in for a period of delayed shock."

She looked into those dark and narrowed eyes.

"Could it be," she asked at length, "that you're a little worried about the extent of the damage you've done to me?"

At this, spoken with a sort of acid sweetness, his eyes widened, and the gravity in his voice gave way to an inflection of chipped ice.

"Be very careful," he warned. "You're my prisoner and as such you'll speak to me with respect – the utmost respect," he added darkly.

Kim fingered her glass, temper rising within her. But caution prevailed as she dwelt on her position. Apart from the initial assault – which was undoubtedly forgivable – he had as yet done her no real harm, and Kim very sensibly decided that, for the present at least, she would endeavour to adopt a conciliatory manner towards him. With her returning lucidity of mind had come the idea that even if she failed to impress him with her story – when of course she was allowed to relate it to him again – she could surely still escape whatever fate he had planned for her. Once on the island she should without too much difficulty be able to conjure up one of her "unorthodox notions" and use it profitably in effecting an escape.

"I don't think I spoke with disrespect," she murmured on realizing he was awaiting some comment from her.

Damon Souris allowed the matter to drop as he told her to drink the rest of her medicine. She obeyed and he took the glass from her. "You can get dressed," he told her, "and then go into the galley and help with the meal."

His abrupt order brought fire to her eye, but she averted her head so that he should not see.

"What time is it?" she asked as the thought occurred to her.

"Almost noon."

"How long is it since – since . . .?" She looked up questioningly.

"Since I rendered you unconscious? About fifteen hours."

"I've been unconscious that long?" she frowned.

"You were coming round late last night. As I'd no intention of having my rest disturbed I poured something down your throat –" He broke off, laughing as she gave a convulsive shudder. "It kept you quiet for rather longer than I expected."

Kim changed the subject.

"Did we sail from Piraeus?"

"Correct." He put up a hand to stifle a yawn, a gesture that irritated Kim beyond all reason. She was not used to being treated to a display of affected boredom by the people with whom she conversed. "I'll leave you to get dressed," he said, and a moment later she was staring at the closed door of the cabin, wondering at the strange sensation that was slowly creeping into her consciousness.

Having dressed herself she came from the cabin on to a narrow, thickly-carpeted deck off which several doors opened. One, a wide double door, had windows through which Kim saw the outer deck. Damon Souris was sitting in the sun, reading a newspaper. He had changed to shorts and these were the full extent of his clothing. His body was bronzed and hard-muscled, his shoulders straight and aristocratic, the hands holding the newspaper long and slender with tapering fingers – sensitive, mused Kim, rather like a surgeon's. She moved away as she saw his head begin to turn. Had he sensed she was there, looking out at him? Kim frowned to herself at the idea. She sincerely hoped he had *not* been aware of her interest. Having found the bathroom she took a warm refreshing bath, and after dressing again she opened a cabinet in search of a comb, found one, washed it under the tap, and proceeded to use it. But her hair, having been fouled by the dirty water of the pool, was matted together and she actually cried out on trying to comb the back, where the huge swelling was. Damon Souris had ordered her to help with the lunch, but she decided to wash

41

her hair instead. Whoever was preparing the food would have had to manage if she had not been here, so he could manage now.

That was better, she thought with relief when after her shampoo she looked in the mirror as she drew the comb through her hair. At least one part of her was normal ... but her face! On examining it Kim began fearfully to wonder if she would be marked for life. That blow must have had tremendous force behind it; Damon Souris didn't intend affording his victim an opportunity of recovering from it and coming back at him. What were his thoughts, Kim wondered, when on the lightning turn he made, he saw the size of his captor? She would scarcely come to his shoulder. Would he have shown a little mercy and pulled his punch if it had been at all possible? – which it was not, of course, because the punch was already on its way before he turned his body, speed being essential with a gun trained on him – as he had believed it to be. Kim felt sure he would have pulled the punch had he known it was a woman walking there behind him; perhaps he would not have fetched a blow at all, but merely knocked the "gun" into the air, as she now felt sure he had done, while delivering the blow with the other hand.

The delicious smell of meat cooking assailed her nostrils as she emerged from the bathroom and she soon found the galley. A man was standing by the stove; he turned as she entered and she saw that it was not the man who had done her washing.

"Can I help?" she began, feeling strangely tensed and nervous and wishing she had disobeyed the command to come along and assist. "I know you must be almost finished, but if I can do some little thing?"

The man, a stocky Greek with two prominent gold

fillings, gave her a smile which was more like a prurient smirk and Kim felt her colour rise. What were these men thinking? – but there really was no need for conjecture about that!

"The table – if you wish, madam – you can prepare it."

"Very well," she said coldly. "Where is the table?"

"I show you, madam. Come this way, please." He led the way into a beautifully-appointed saloon with wide windows leading on to a verandah. A dining-table stood in the centre; the cutlery and cloth were in the drawer, he told her, and went out, leaving her to spend a couple of minutes or so in admiration of her surroundings. Damon Souris must be inordinately wealthy; and she dwelt again on his conviction that he was being abducted for the ransom his safe return to his family would bring. His family.... Hitherto she had not thought of them, but now she wondered if he had a wife and children, then swiftly dismissed the idea. No married man would take a woman to his home – and it was to his home she was going ... unless she could escape or, better still, make him listen to her.

Without thinking Kim set two places at the table, and she was a little puzzled when, on entering the saloon twenty minutes later, clad in white again but in a shirt this time instead of a sweater, Damon stood stock still in the doorway and regarded the table from under arrogantly-raised eyebrows.

"Who's laid this?" he wanted to know, transferring his gaze to her face.

"I did. Isn't it right?"

"I wasn't expecting company for lunch. Who's the other place for?"

Kim flushed scarlet at his sarcasm. With the total

43

clearing of the mist that had impaired her clarity of thought, and in consequence had brought about a meekness in her bred in part from her contrition at the mistake she had made, there was a partial return of her innate strength of character, and her fearlessness. She had taken quite a lot from this arrogant foreigner, but there was a limit. True, he was the injured party, with every right to be angry, but as Kim was not the cheap little crook he assumed her to be, she was becoming a little tired of being so branded. All that was necessary for a full clearing up of the situation was for him to listen to her for just about five minutes, for him to accept in fact what she had already told him, but in his arrogance he refused to budge from his conviction that he was the intended victim of a female gang of kidnappers. Stubborn man!

"I'm sorry," she said in stiff constrained tones, her chin tilted and her eye alight. "I took it for granted that I also should be partaking of some food." Fury simmered while caution strove to turn off the heat.

"Most certainly you shall eat . . . in the galley."

Kim drew a deep breath, choking back the impulse to retaliate. Damon Souris came slowly into the saloon, and stood close to her, too close for her liking and she stepped back. "I don't sit at the same table with cheap and nasty little crooks." An imperious flick of his hand was a gesture towards the door. "Out," he ordered her softly, "and don't let me find you in here again."

Kim's fists clenched; the light in her eye became almost luminous. A little voice inside her said that she should remember to make excuses for him, that a man of his obvious position and culture would naturally view with distaste the idea of sitting down to eat with a crook. But that little voice was ignored as Kim said in accents quivering with fury,

"If I'm so contaminating to you, and to this –" her hand flashed in a scornful gesture, "this expensive toy, then what induced you bring me aboard? Why didn't you leave me where I was?"

An awful silence dropped. Staring at him, she was vexed to find herself tingling with apprehension at the change in him, the complete transformation in his manner from one of rather mild disdain to one of smouldering fury. Deep crimson tinged his face and his eyes kindled, dark and glowering. She noted the tightly drawn lips, the taut jaw. Redoubtable he looked and every inch a Greek with his bronzed skin and low brow, with those firm classical features and hawk-like eyes and nose. Kim moistened her lips and told herself it would have been better to have left out the bit about the "toy".

"What induced me?" he snarled. "Retaliation! I've already said no female threatens me and gets away with it. By the time I've finished with you you'll wish with all your heart that I had left you in that pool to drown! You enjoyed yourself jabbing that gun into my back, but by heaven you'll regret it! And now, if you know what's good for you you'll get out of here – for otherwise I might not wait until I get you to my home!"

Wait for what? she asked herself as she made her way unsteadily to the door. The man was a devil, and his intentions evil. Was he intending to torture her, or put her into solitary confinement, or what?

As such conjecture was totally unprofitable she put it from her, but her appetite had gone and she went back to the cabin which she presumed she was to occupy while the trip lasted. She stood by the dressing-table staring at her reflection, and cringing at what she

45

saw. How long would it take that eye to get back to normal? she wondered, fingering it tenderly. And the bump on the back of her head. . . . It was a wonder her brain had not been affected, she thought, and unreasoning anger rose against the man out there, lunching alone, in the splendour of the saloon. What had been his business in Athens? And why was he at the Imperial? That he had been staying there she was now fairly certain. He had shaved not long before entering the car. Was it his car? Kim rather thought it might have been hired, since it was most unlikely he would have a car in Athens if he lived on Cos. Of course, he could have a home in the city; many business men did, as well as having homes on the islands. Why the devil did it have to be a black Mercedes! And why, since it *was* a black Mercedes, did it have to be parked there – not quite where Takis was supposed to park, but near enough for the mistake to have occurred? Kim heaved a sigh and sat down on the bed. What a mess she was in, and all because of Diana's foolishness. How was she to extricate herself? And if she failed to think up some way of escape, just how long would she be kept on the island?

She *would* think of some way of escape! It was not possible that she could be kept a prisoner. Yet she envisaged almost insuperable difficulties ahead once she had escaped. She had neither money nor clothes – apart from those she stood up in, the black trews and sweater. She might get by without any more, but she could not hope to get very far without money. Once she was free she could go to the police, of course, but what sort of a story was she going to tell them? Whatever she said must inevitably sound highly suspicious and illogical.

At last Kim threw off every thought apertaining to

her predicament; it was all too infinitely depressing. Going out on to the deck where she had seen Damon Souris sitting, she stood by the rail, looking out over the sea. Islands could be discerned, gleaming in the sunshine. How long would they be reaching Cos? she wondered. Cos. . . . It was a pretty island, she had read, and was full of antiquities –

She turned, nerves tingling.

"I hope you don't mind my taking a breath of fresh air?" she said, anticipating an order for her to remove herself from the deck where he was perhaps intending to sit.

"The air's free," he replied unexpectedly, and sat down on a luxuriously-padded deck chair.

"When will we arrive at Cos?" she asked.

"At about six this evening."

"So soon?" She looked at him in surprise. He was facing her and she felt his intense scrutiny on her face, taking in her disfigurement. Involuntarily she half-turned, so that her undamaged side was towards him.

"So soon," he repeated, and added, "You don't seem to appreciate the seriousness of your situation."

"Certainly I do. I don't understand why you should say that."

He studied her profile.

"You're not as afraid as you should be under the circumstances."

She turned, forgetful for the moment of her disfigurement.

"I'm no coward, if that was what you were expecting."

Curiously he said,

"Have you any idea what you're in for?"

"None at all. I don't expect you'll torture me."

"I'm quite capable of it."

47

Kim examined his featuress; there certainly was a ruthless quality about them, but she was remembering her earlier impression that there was a contradictory element in his make-up, and she was also, for no apparent reason at all, remembering the strange sensation that had crept over her a short while ago after Damon had left her cabin.

"I can't imagine your doing so."

His head tilted.

"No? Why?" he asked in an odd voice.

"Because I cannot imagine what form the torture would take."

"Merely locking you up would be torture to a woman like you, who is used to having a good time – n the proceeds of your crimes."

She was on the point of telling him that she worked for a living, but refrained, held back by an inexplicable reluctance to bring about a change in his mood. She knew a strange disinclination to see that sardonic expression on his face, that sneer of contempt on his mouth, reflecting his disbelief of what she said.

"I shall be reported missing," she said, veering the subject a little.

"By whom?"

"My two friends."

"Confederates," he corrected smoothly, and Kim gave a resigned shrug of her shoulders.

"If that's what you prefer to call them." He said nothing and she added, "They'll have gone to the police by now."

"No such thing. As I've said, they'd have taken to their heels once they realized something had gone wrong."

Kim let that pass without comment.

"What exactly are your intentions?" she inquired,

feeling he might be a little more expansive, in this present mood.

"Regarding what?"

Kim moistened her lips. She just had to know what was in store for her, should she fail in her attempts at escape.

"What are you going to do with me?"

To her surprise a strange sort of silence followed this. She stared down into his aristocratic face and with a little catch of breath realized that he was at a loss for words! At a loss – after all those subtle hints and warnings? Could it possibly be that although he had been endeavouring to put fear into her, he was in fact not quite sure just what to do with her? Bewildered and astounded by this impression, she dwelt on it for a space. At the time he had abducted her he was in a most furious rage, and it required little imagination on Kim's part to see him, driven by this wrath, bundling her into the car and carrying her off to where his yacht was berthed, and to where he was obviously proceeding when the piece of wood was thrust in his back and he was ordered to change his course. His intention had been to punish her severely for her audacity in holding him up – him, the proud and noble Damon Souris who, it would appear, was a man of substance. What form of punishment he would inflict on his captive Damon in his blind rage would not have been able to decide, or even envisage.

The more she pondered it the more Kim became convinced that the abduction was done on impulse and she did wonder, were it possible to read his mind, whether she would discover that he was actually regretting having abducted her at all – that he was wishing heartily he had left her where she was. Her spirits soared, for if these deductions were correct then assuredly he would free her without much delay, glad to be rid of her, as she had now become a nuisance. Viewing her position in the light of these conclusions, Kim listened without much interest to what he had to say, since she surmised they were merely idle threats he was about to voice.

"For a start I shall lock you up. That should afford you the opportunity of deciding whether or not it was a good idea to poke a gun between my shoulders."

"Lock me up?" she repeated calmly, ignoring his second sentence completely. "How long for?"

He regarded her with a frowning expression.

"You appear quite insensible of your danger. Perhaps your brain's not yet cleared sufficiently for you to grasp the situation properly?"

"My brain's quite clear, thank you."

His black eyes narrowed; there was danger in their depths. But the man was extremely puzzled also, puzzled by her calm dignity and lack of fear.

"Cowards usually become cringing little rats when the showdown approaches and punishment is within sight."

"I've just said, I'm not a coward." Her chin went up; but then she remembered her disfigurement and felt she must be an object of amusement to the self-assured man sitting there, looking like the acme of some sculpture's perfection. She waited, during the silence that followed, expecting some caustic rejoinder. It was with an inner gasp of amazement that she heard him say, in a voice that had lost its cutting edge entirely,

"No . . . strangely, you are not. You possess a certain strength and power not normally found in women." But then he added, as if impelled to, "Had you been a little more clever you'd have made a successful crook, and a genteel one."

Kim couldn't help saying,

"Am I to take that as flattery, Mr. Souris?"

"It was a fact; I make a point of never flattering a woman." She said nothing and he added, "What's your name? I saw a 'K' on the handkerchief I took out of your pocket."

She told him and he repeated it.

"Kim Lyttleton. Miss, I take it?"

"That's right."

"How old are you?"

"Twenty-three."

"Twenty-three. . . ." He looked her over, from her deep auburn hair to her high forehead and widely-spaced eyes, to the exquisite arch of her neck and lower. His gaze lingered a little insolently before moving to her tiny waist and then down to her ankles, just visible below the bottom of her trews. "Hmm. . . ." He appeared to have had an idea. "You might be quite presentable when your blemishes are healed."

She frowned at him.

"What has my appearance to do with anything?" she inquired innocently, and a curve touched the fine outline of his lips.

"If it comes up to my requirements I might take you for my pillow friend."

"Your — *what*?" she asked, face flaming.

"It would be quite handy to have one permanently in the house. Yes, I rather think you might be of use to me after all." He laughed at her expression, and her blushes. "You're a surprising girl, Kim Lyttleton, and a puzzling one. Or is this air of outraged innocence all an act? I feel sure that in your particular line of business you must have had your moments . . . with some of the thugs you're used to mixing with. Still, it will

51

all add spice. I abhor inexperienced women, as I am sure you abhor inexperienced men." His dark eyes raked her insultingly. "We should get along famously – that is, of course, if your looks satisfy me."

"You're despicable!" Kim's own glance did some raking and she saw his eyes narrow dangerously. But she was in a fury and nothing short of a gag could have stopped her tongue. "I was willing to adopt a suitable amount of contrition and humility, because of the inconvenience I caused you, accepting your insults and making allowances for them, but I've had enough! I've taken all I'm going to take and if it's war you want then war it shall be! Your arrogance and your swagger and flourish are not only deplorable, they're pathetic! If you could see yourself as others see you then perhaps you'd drop a little of your conceit! And as for my becoming your – your – pillow friend, let me warn you that I'm not such a weakling that I couldn't put up a fight – a good one!" She stopped, and winced as a pain shot through her eyes. "You might be able to use your fists, but I can use my fingernails, and as a matter of fact I'd enjoy doing so. I'd thoroughly enjoy seeing *your* face disfigured!" As she spoke it had registered that his expression was taking on a murderous aspect and, feeling suddenly drained – for no reason that she could see at the moment – she decided that retreat was the better course and, turning, she would have left the deck. But without warning her hair was grabbed and she was brought to an abrupt halt. A small scream escaped her as a spasm of sheer agony shot through her head, for he had made a grab at the hair covering the swelling. Twisting round with a lightning move, she let out and kicked him on the shin. To her immense satisfaction she saw him wince, but the twist had caused her some pain too, since she had

52

dragged her hair from his grasp in making it. Tears came on to her cheeks, but she brushed them away angrily, hoping he had not been quick enough to notice them.

"You – damned spitfire!" he snarled, glaring at her. "I'll shake you till you cry for mercy!"

Kim moved backwards, but he was upon her and she felt her arms taken in a vicious grip. Before he had time to carry out his threat she had kicked him again; this time she had the satisfaction of seeing him catch his lip at the pain, and then she saw no more. . . .

CHAPTER FOUR

KIM was trembling from head to foot. "Delayed shock," said a curt voice as she opened her eyes. That detestable man stood there, at the other side of the saloon, his dark head outlined against the window.

"No such thing!" she denied, rallying despite her throbbing head. "You caused it – making a grab at my hair like that. Have you no sense at all?"

Damon took a deep breath, then his lips compressed. His manner was cold rather than wrathful and even before he spoke she had the impression that he was wishing with all his heart that he had left her where she was.

"If you know what's good for you, my girl, you'll hold your tongue. I've been put to enough trouble with you already and I'm not tolerating your impertinence into the bargain. *I* say it's delayed shock – and delayed shock it is!" To Kim's amazement he pushed a hand through his hair in a gesture of asperity. He looked harassed beyond measure and despite the way she felt her spirits rose. She was convinced that it was only a matter of time before he set her free, glad to be rid of the encumbrance.

It was going dark when at last the harbour of Cos was sighted; the lights looked pretty and as the yacht came in closer delightful scents assailed Kim's nostrils. A medley of small boats of all colours filled the picturesque port, which was too small for the berthing of large liners. From a café somewhere along the flower-bedecked waterfront *bouzouki* music floated over the smooth dark water. Still shaky and shivering, Kim had no desire to make any protest when, once ashore, she was bustled unceremoniously into a waiting car. The dark stocky driver stared at her expressionlessly as he held open the door through which she was pushed by her captor. Was he used to his employer's bringing home young ladies? she wondered, then grimaced as she tried to imagine his thoughts on noticing her face. He would not be used to seeing this sort of girl, that was for sure!

A drive along a tree-lined avenue, then along a few miles of more lonely road, brought them to the undulating base of the mountain and within a few minutes the car was being brought to a halt outside a low rambling villa surrounded by sub-tropical gardens from which heady perfumes filled the evening air.

A maid appeared and was told to show Kim up to a guest room.

"Yes, Mr. Damon." Elene's dark eyes fluttered surreptitiously over Kim's black-clad figure before settling on her face, any surprise being concealed under an expressionless mask similar to that of the driver of the car. Damon Souris's staff were well trained, thought Kim when after showing her the room Elene silently withdrew, closing the door behind her.

For a long moment Kim stood pensively in the

centre of the room, thinking of these two servants she had met and feeling sure that they must talk together, later, about the oddly-dressed English girl with the scarred face, who brought no clothes except those in which she stood up.

The bed, satin-covered and large, was inviting, but Kim went over to the window and looked out into the garden. Another car was just arriving; a man hurriedly left it and went towards the patio on which, it would appear, Damon Souris was standing, for the man spoke immediately. Silently opening the window, just an inch or so, Kim listened to the conversation taking place between the two men. Or at least she listened to part of it, as now and then the newcomer would speak in Greek. Damon Souris would then reply in Greek, but so much was spoken in English that Kim had not the slightest difficulty in absorbing the whole of the situation. Damon Souris's mother, of whom he appeared to be inordinately fond, had been taken ill and rushed to hospital where it was discovered she had a brain tumour. There was no hope of recovery and Damon, shocked, and speaking in a broken voice, said he would go to the hospital immediately. However, he was stopped by the other man who said that Damon's mother had asked that her son's English fiancée come to the hospital with him, as she wanted to see her before she died.

"She knows she's dying?" Damon's voice was vibrant with emotion, and in spite of her dislike of him Kim felt a surge of compassion sweep over her.

"She seems to have guessed. And all she wants is to see Suzanne and be sure that you've got yourself a nice girl at last. She's never approved of your wicked ways, you know, Damon."

A small silence and then,

"I haven't brought Suzanne back with me."

55

"You —! But that was why you went to England — to bring her over and present her to the family."

"We quarrelled," Damon explained briefly.

"You don't appear to be very upset about it," the other man commented curiously.

"I'm too concerned about Mother. . . ." A small silence and then, "I obviously can't tell her that Suzanne and I have quarrelled. I shall think of something as I go along. I must leave you, Nico —"

"Damon . . . your mother will be quick to notice if you lie. Even I know that's it's virtually impossible to deceive her, and I'm only her nephew. You as her son should know better than to believe you can deceive her. Is the engagement off?" Nico went on to add, and after a small pause Damon admitted that it was. "What happened?" Nico then asked, and all Damon would say was that they had discovered they weren't suited. "Not suited!" exclaimed Nico. "Isn't it a bit late to discover that?"

"Look, Nico, I'm not wasting time explaining my private affairs to you. I'm going to Mother right away."

Kim drew back as Damon went towards the car. Nico followed and she heard him say,

"Aunt Maroula will be heartbroken. I was with her an hour ago and she said she would die happy only if she knew your future was settled. She wasn't really in favour of your becoming engaged to an English girl, if you remember, but she abided by it. And I think the fact that Suzanne was at college, and seriously studying for her teacher's certificate, helped to assuage any fears she might have had that the girl would not prove a suitable wife for you. Aunt Maroula admires studious people, as you know." Kim looked out and saw Nico shake his head. "What a tragedy that you couldn't bring the girl back with you."

Suddenly Damon stopped in his tracks, and glanced towards Kim's window.

"I have an idea!" he said in tense and vibrant tones. "Nico, go home and get a dress of Katrina's, and a coat – yes, a coat! Hurry!"

"But ... a dress and coat of my sister's? Damon, what –?"

"Go, Nico, and ask questions later!" And without waiting for any further argument from his cousin cousin Damon strode back to the patio. Kim saw him take the steps at a couple of agile leaps, her heart pounding and her head beginning to throb again.

She was standing by the bed, her face pale and her hands clenched, when without ceremony Damon entered the room.

"You," he began without preamble, "get your face and hands washed. You're coming with me!"

She swallowed, clearing her throat in preparation to telling him she had been listening and she had not the slightest intention of carrying out his wishes. But something about his face – the stricken expression it carried, and the greyness at the corners of his mouth – checked the intended refusal and instead she feigned surprise and asked,

"Where to?"

"The hospital. My mother's –" Emotion cut short the rest, emotion which seemed totally out of place in so strong a man as Damon Souris undoubtedly was. "My mother's dangerously ill," he continued presently. "She wants to see my fiancée before – before she dies. You must impersonate her – No, don't ask questions," he snapped as Kim opened her mouth. "I'll explain all you need to know on the way to the hospital." He thumbed towards a door which, Kim had already surmised, led to a bathroom. "My cousin's gone to get you some clothes. Tidy up as best you can – in there." He looked frowningly at her disfigured face. "I'll tell Mother you had a fall – and don't you dare deny it, or anything else I say. Get me?"

Kim gritted her teeth. The man was asking a favour and yet he adopted this dictatorial manner. She couldn't help retorting,

"And supposing I do deny things you say?" and instantly wished she hadn't exhibited such temerity, for with a sudden leap he was close and before she knew what was happening she felt the strength of his fingers on her throat.

"I'll strangle you when I get you back!" he snarled, and released her, watching her swallow convulsively as she tried to ease the muscles, and the pain. "And at the hospital," he added darkly as he read her thoughts, "if you so much as dare ask anyone's aid, or mention what has happened to you, I'll immediately call the police and hand you over to them. Now," he ordered, "in there, and make yourself as presentable as possible!"

Kim obeyed without further delay, lifting a soothing hand to her throat. The man was a savage, a demoniacal brute who, she decided, would not stop at murder, should murder be necessary for the furthering of any scheme he might happen to have in mind.

True to his word, he gave her a brief explanation as they drove along to the hospital. She learned little more than had been conveyed to her by her eavesdropping, but she listened without comment, merely expressing suitable words of sympathy on hearing him say that his mother had a brain tumour. She was a widow and had lived a few miles from her son, in a pretty village nestling at the foot of Mount Dikalos. For some time she had wanted to see him settled down and now she desired to see the girl to whom he had become engaged some months ago when he was on one of his business trips to England. His mouth would repeatedly set as he continued and Kim knew that he hated having to impart these details to her. However, they were necessary, and he continued by saying that his engagement was broken. Kim must remember that her name was Suzanne and, finally, he said that although his mother had seen snapshots of Suzanne she would probably not have remembered much about her appearance, and in any case, Kim's disfigurements would prevent his mother from discovering the differences. Damon then fell silent and for the rest of the journey neither of them spoke.

Mrs. Souris, very dark with deep-set eyes, looked to be about sixty years of age. On Damon's introducing her she took Kim's hand in hers and uttered a great sigh of relief. The two took to one another instantly and Kim found herself swallowing a painful little lump in her throat at the idea that the woman was soon going to die.

"Suzanne. . . ." Mrs. Souris looked at her face and frowned, but Damon quickly explained about the "fall". "Poor child! Does it hurt?"

"Not now," answered Kim, although that was by no means the truth.

"Your hair? Damon dear, Suzanne's hair was blonde on the coloured snapshots you showed me — very blonde, I remember."

He nodded, at the same time shooting a warning glance at Kim, telling her to keep silent.

"She had on a wig, darling. Girls do wear them, as you know, and Suzanne has several."

Another frown.

"You shouldn't, dear, not with hair like that. It's

59

very lovely. Promise me you won't cover it up with nasty false hair."

Kim smiled.

"I promise," she said, withdrawing her hand as Mrs. Souris released it.

"Well, darling," Damon was saying a short while later, "are you quite satisfied with my fiancée?" His voice was light but, watching the movement in his throat, Kim knew what it was costing him to keep it so. "You're perfectly happy now?"

Both to Damon's surprise and Kim's there was silence for a long while after he had put his questions.

"I think, Damon, that I would like to see you married before I go."

"*Married?*" echoed Kim involuntarily, and received a most darkling glance from the man who had abducted her.

"Is there any reason why you shouldn't be married right away?" The direct question was put to Kim, and she knew it was owing to her unthinking ejaculation. She looked at Damon, saw that he was at a loss for words and as something had to be found in answer to Mrs. Souris's question Kim said the only thing she could say, under the circumstances, and hoped Damon would clear up the whole position later.

"Well, no, not really."

"Of course there isn't." Mrs. Souris smiled and looked at her son. "You did say, dear, that you and Suzanne were only waiting for her to finish her studies, and as she has now done so I see no cause for further delay." She paused and lines appeared in her brow, also little beads of perspiration. Kim glanced at Damon; he was watching his mother's face intently, his own features grey and drawn. It was clear that Mrs. Souris was now experiencing some pain. "I shall be happy only when I see you married to this charming girl."

Another glance cast at Damon, and this time Kim went a trifle red, for mingling with the shadows in his eyes was a distinctly dry expression. Charming girl. . . . What would his mother say were she to learn that in his eyes Kim was nothing but a shady little crook?

"Well, Mother," Damon began, but was instantly interrupted.

"We don't have long engagements here, so you shall be married at once. It isn't as if Suzanne has obligations back home; you've told me all about her and she hasn't any relatives to speak of – an aunt, you mentioned, I think?"

Both Kim and Damon remained silent for a space. Had the situation not been so tragic it would have been decidedly funny, thought Kim, wondering what Damon's thoughts were and whether he were dwelling on what sort of wife she would make. Not that he was contemplating marriage, she thought with an inward grimace. The whole situation was like something out of a play; it was fiction, not fact. Kim allowed her mind to wander to this Suzanne: she wondered what she was like – in fact, she was extremely curious about her, since it would be interesting to discover just what kind of a girl appealed to the austere and unpredictable Damon Souris.

He was speaking, reminding his mother that his fiancée had really come only on a visit, in order to meet his family. He and she hadn't thought of getting married quite so soon. Suzanne had to return to her own country in order to settle her affairs. He continued in this persuasive vein for a while and, musing on his attitude it did seem to Kim that neither he nor this Suzanne had been over-keen to enter the blissful state of marriage. Of course, the girl had been finishing her studies, but somehow, on what small knowledge she had of Damon, Kim would have wagered her last penny on his being the sort of man who, having asked a girl to be his wife, would immediately demand an early wedding. He was naturally dictatorial, masterful. He would command and his fiancée obey. Obviously he had not been in a hurry to relinquish his freedom, and this seemed a definite pointer to the fact that he had never been in love with the girl. In addition, his manner had revealed not the slightest sign of the distress which would have been expected in a man whose engagement had just been broken. It would seem that he was not in the least perturbed about it, she decided, watching his face as he smiled tenderly down at his mother. What a change in his features! Gone was every vestige of austerity and Kim scarcely recognized the dark and fiendish Greek who so recently had threatened to strangle her. His mother looked into his eyes for a long moment before saying,

"I haven't much time, Damon –"

"Mother," he cut in despairingly, uncaring for the moment of his loss of pride before Kim, "don't talk like that!"

"Damon," she said slowly and emphatically, "let us not pretend. Neither Nico nor the doctor, nor any of the others, has told me anything, in spite of my asking. I *know,* my son, that I have only about a week – perhaps not that; I might have less. The very fact that this thing is inoperable provides proof and enough that I am going to die – Don't look like that, child. I've carried a great sadness ever since your father died, and much as I love you I shall not mind going. But I want to see you settled; I want to know that you're going to be happy, and have a wife and children, just as any man should." Damon turned away and on noticing the sudden clenching of his fist Kim realized just what mental agony he was going through. "Suzanne," his mother was saying, "are you willing to marry my son immediately?"

Lord, what a predicament! Kim could only stare at Damon, silently telling him to answer for her. But he seemed incapable of finding an answer, which was understandable, and for what seemed an age silence hung between the three, with Mrs. Souris looking most oddly at her son, and he standing there desperately trying to produce something that would satisfy her, while Kim herself was so caught up in the drama that nothing else in her life seemed of the smallest measure of importance. A million miles seemed to separate her from Mumsie and Pauline and Enid; her home and her work were vague and unreal elements; the abduction of Damon had occurred a long, long time ago. "Why are you both so silent? Why are you showing so little enthusiasm for marriage?" Fear and uncertainty and suspicion were all mingled in the woman's voice and an instant denial was wrung from her son in his urgency to assuage her doubts.

"No such thing, darling. Suzanne and I are more than eager to get married."

"Then why must you delay?" came the swift inquiry, spoken in a challenging tone.

Damon's eyes held the most odd expression as they met those of Kim; she felt a quiver run through her body, but as yet it was too vague for complete recognition.

"We'll discuss it, Mother," he promised, but she was not to be put off by this.

"Damon, I want an answer now. If you want me to

die happy then accede to my request for an immediate wedding – I'd like you to be married here, in this room, where I can witness it."

Damon sent Kim another strange glance; this time she gave an inward gasp and stiffened apprehensively. Surely he wasn't about to make a promise which it would be impossible for him to keep! Her eyes warned, but his own eyes merely narrowed, in a determined sort of way.

"That was most unkind of you," she was saying immediately they had left the room and the door had closed behind them. "Your mother's going to be put to unnecessary suffering. I can't think what made you make a promise that could never be carried out."

Damon said, very quietly,

"The promise will be carried out."

"*What!*" They had begun to walk along the corridor, but Kim stopped, brought up sharply by his calm but emphasized statement. She stood, transfixed, and stared up into his dark inflexible features. "You must be out of your mind!"

"My mind has never been clearer," he said in smooth and even tones, "nor my intention more firm."

The man was mad! she decided, endeavouring to frame a response but finding herself so enveloped in amazement that she was dumbfounded. And at that moment the doctor appeared and on opening his mouth to say something to Damon, whom he knew by sight, he changed his mind and asked Kim what had happened to her.

"I had a fall," she said as the doctor pulled down the flesh from around her eye. His glance went to the swelling on the back of her head.

"Did you fall on your face or your back?" he inquired curiously.

"On my – on my face," she stammered, hoping to receive some assistance from Damon, but failing. He was so preoccupied that he scarcely took any notice of the doctor at all.

"Then how," the doctor wanted to know, "did you receive the injury to your head?"

Kim moistend her lips, searching for some feasible explanation. But with her mind dazed anyway she failed utterly and merely said, resigned to the fact of its absurdity,

"I fell twice, once on my face and then on my back."

"You did?" with widening eyes and an edge of disbelief to his tone. "How extraordinary." Kim said nothing, but merely coloured guiltily. "Well, if that is what you say. . . . You had better come along with me and let me have a good look at you. That head must be X-rayed."

Half an hour later Kim was in the car with Damon, being driven home from the hospital, a box of ointment in her bag and also tablets for the pain. Her eye had been treated with some sort of lotion and it was now half open; the cut above it had been cleansed and a dressing applied. She felt much better physically, but her mind was in chaos. After he had finished with her the doctor had spoken to Damon, in her hearing.

"I was passing the door," he said, "and could not help overhearing your mother's request for you to get married. It will make her happy; I hope you will carry out her wish?"

"It is our intention to do so," was Damon's calm response, and the doctor's severe mouth had relaxed in a smile.

"This is very good. I like and admire your mother.

She is brave, for she has guessed that she is reaching the end, and yet she bears up so well ... yes, she is brave, and I am glad indeed that she will know this happiness before she dies."

Kim spoke no word in the car, and neither did her companion. She turned her head once or twice, to cast him a sideways glance. His profile was set and hard, his jaw out-thrust in the most formidable line. Kim tried to dismiss her growing fears, telling herself that they were utterly stupid. But this man was so unpredictable, and she soon became conscious of the most disquieting premonition. It was utterly ridiculous and illogical to feel like this, she told herself angrily. She could not be forced into marriage! In any case, she was just about the last person Damon would want to marry, no matter how great his anxiety for his mother. He had something in mind, she repeatedly assured herself ... and the next moment she was wondering what he *could* have in mind. There was nothing that she could visualize, and, because the matter was becoming more and more troublesome to her, she determinedly pushed it away from her consciousness. But it returned with startling reality the moment they had entered the villa.

"I meant what I said." Damon's voice was a very strange mixture of reluctance and determination. He hated the very idea of marrying her, yet his chief concern was for his mother's peace of mind. "I know what you're about to say, but you can save your breath. I intend—"

"Save my breath!" she interrupted incredulously. "Are you quite mad? I haven't the slightest intention of listening to such rubbish!"

"You'll not only listen, you'll act ... as I order." Soft the words, but there was no mistaking the authority they carried, and that disquieting sensation flooded over Kim once more, much stronger this time so that it almost savoured of a fear, vivid and intense.

"You're talking in the most irrational way," she told him, angry at her own confusion of mind. "You can't make me marry you."

They were both standing in the living-room – Damon by the window and Kim still by the door, where she had stayed, with the intention of stating her intention of going to the bedroom allotted to her and lying down.

"I *can* make you." Damon's dark eyes fixed her gaze. "You know the position – that it is desperate. Either you marry me or I hand you over to the poilce."

Silence. How could she have forgotten this ace he held? Were she to be handed over to the police she would be in for a bad time, a period of trial and imprisonment. Mumsie would be informed; she would blame herself. . . .

"You're blackmailing me?" she said, and saw his dark brows come together in a frown.

"That's a most unpleasant word," he snapped, and Kim's rejoinder came at once,

"This is a most unpleasant situation. You can't possibly want to marry me."

"Marry *you*?" His lip curled. "A third-rate crook? No, certainly I don't want to marry you!"

Kim's cheeks coloured with anger.

"In that case," she returned in choking accents, "there's nothing more to be said!"

His hand flicked with a gesture of exasperation.

"Stop procrastinating, girl! As I've told you, either you'll marry me or take the rap for your crime. I must warn you that our police take a pretty poor view of crimes of violence. Severe penalties are meted out – especially to foreigners who enter our country with the intention of holding up its citizens with guns."

"I didn't have a gun."

Damon's face twisted with impatience.

"Let's keep to the point. My ultimatum is: you marry me or you shall be handed over to the police. You could get a stretch of ten years," he added, and was gratified to see the colour leave her face.

"Ten years?" she faltered, overwhelmed by the natural human trait of fear of confinement. "I d-don't believe you."

"No? I think you do. Make up your mind, Kim Lyttleton – and make it up quickly." He meant business; the gleam in his eye plainly warned that he made no idle threats. Without the least vestige of doubt Kim knew that if she refused to do as he wished he would be so furious that he would not hesitate to hand her over to the police as an act of revenge, despite his earlier statement about not wanting the publicity. There was a satanic quality about him, a sort of pagan love for his mother, whose peace of mind was his sole concern. Should Kim hold out, and his mother die unhappy, he would show no mercy to the girl responsible. "You'll be free in a week's time. . . ." He allowed his firm voice to fade; Kim noted the stark anguish in his face and in spite of her hatred for him she knew a stab of compassion also. However harsh his nature, whatever pagan traits he possessed – and Kim was sure he possessed a good many – he had a deep abiding love for his mother; this much Kim did allow in his favour.

"Free in a week?" She gave him a direct look. "And in the meantime?" she challenged, recalling all too vividly his remarks about making her his pillow friend. She rather thought, though, that he would be far too occupied with his mother to trouble himself

68

about more sensual pursuits.

"What exactly do you mean?" he inquired in clipped and formal tones.

"I think you know."

His dark eyes glinted.

"Explain," he commanded sharply.

"I shall be left alone?" she then said bluntly, and received a glance of contempt which brought the colour to her cheeks.

"Severely alone," he replied, his glance taking in the whole of her body with the same expression of contempt that had set her blushing. "And now, have you reached a decision?"

"Afterwards . . . there will be a divorce?"

"I expect you'll be able to get one in your own country. Here, we don't treat marriage so lightly."

Amazed, she could only stare at him for a space, her own eyes arrogant and faintly contemptuous.

"If this isn't treating marriage lightly then I don't know what is! Two people, detesting one another, entering the state of matrimony simply in order to suit themselves! You want your mother to be happy – at – at the end, while I wish only to escape prosecution. Treat marriage lightly? It's downright abuse, in my opinion!"

Her indignation caught and held his attention. He seemed surprised by it, and a little puzzled. He wouldn't have credited her with ideals, he seemed to be saying. Aloud he said,

"You misunderstood me. What I meant was that I myself do not favour divorce."

"No?" in some surprise. "You're a most extraordinary man, Mr. Souris."

"Simply because I don't favour divorce?"

"Simply because not favouring divorce seems alien

to your character."

"You're in no position to assess my character!"

Kim shrugged her shoulders.

"I'm judging only by what I've learned of you in our short acquaintanceship."

"You've learned nothing. And there's no need for you to waste your time trying to learn anything. Make your decision, that's all you're required to do." Clearly he was furious at the idea of her passing an opinion about his character. Kim gave an impatient little sigh. He believed her to be a crook, so it was excusable that he should resent anything remotely apertaining to the personal. What Kim could not excuse, however, was his adamant attitude in refusing to accept her explanation. Were he to know the truth then all he would have against her was the inconvenience she had caused him — and of course the temporary humiliation. And were he an understanding sort of man he would forgive her instantly, agreeing that the man Takis had deserved to be taught a lesson. But, glancing at his profile as he stood by the window, half turned so that he looked out into the garden, and noting that angular line of his out-thrust jaw, Kim decided that even if he did know the truth he would definitely not be ready and willing to understand, and to forgive. He was not that kind of man.

"Can I have some time to think about this proposition of yours?" she asked at last.

"My ultimatum," he corrected smoothly, at the same time nodding his head in consent. She was told to go to her bedroom, which she readily did. He required her answer in half an hour's time.

Reaching the room, Kim entered and flopped down on the bed, presently discovering to her disgust that tears of self-pity and defeat were hovering close.

What a dreadful mess she was in! Little had she guessed at the result when with blithe disdain for failure she had embarked on the plan which was designed to save her foster-mother from worry. Diana.... Kim could willingly have strangled her!

Half an hour Damon had given her. Half an hour in which to decide between marriage to the arrogant creature or trial and imprisonment. That she had possessed no gun would avail her nothing, since she would not be believed. True, the pond would be dragged, but the fact that no gun was found would not in any way serve as proof that she'd never had one. There was the damning evidence of the tape recorder, which was in Damon's possession and which she could not deny was hers. She would be asked questions, would have to answer truthfully, and those answers would instantly condemn her. She could bring the two girls as witnesses that she had abducted the wrong man, but as the intent was still there the result would merely be the incrimination of Pauline and Enid while benefiting Kim herself precious little, and as the involvement of the two girls was the last thing Kim desired she had to face the fact that she was entirely alone in this. She thought of Mumsie, and the effect it would have on her were she to discover that Kim had landed herself in jail — and all because of her. No, it would not do at all. Her foster-mother was definitely not going to be hurt over this aspect of the affair. She was probably suffering enough already, what with Kim being missing, and of course, Diana's lover being free to contact her and — having denied sending any message regarding a change of time — take her off as originally planned.

With her thoughts flitting about in all directions as she continued to meditate on the factors one by one,

Kim reached the reluctant conclusion that she had no choice other than to marry the detestable Damon Souris. And she was also brought face to face with the truth: she was compelled – not without a deep sense of shock – to admit that she was in fact a criminal; not in her own eyes, of course, but most certainly where the law was concerned. On the surface the situation was perfectly clear; she had held up Damon, forced him by threats to drive where she wanted him to drive; she had pushed something in his back, something which he had naturally believed to be a gun – she had meant him to believe it was a gun. Undoubtedly she would be convicted, and, according to Damon who might or might not be exaggerating a little, she was liable to a sentence of ten years. Most certainly she would receive at least five. Five years in jail. . . . Kim shuddered and glanced at her watch.

The half hour had almost come to an end. . . .

CHAPTER FIVE

IT was only after having made her decision that Kim realized just how awkward it would be to explain her sudden marriage to her foster-mother; and it would be even more difficult finding an explanation for its almost immediate collapse. Kim mentioned this to her husband four days after their marriage. He had just returned from a visit to the hospital, and on noting his expression she experienced an unaccountable access of foreboding. He had entered the living-room of the picturesque and luxuriously-appointed villa and for a long moment stood staring at her from the depths of those dark satanic eyes – or was it through her? she wondered, unable to suppress a shudder. His manner had been baffling for the past two days and several times she had been acutely conscious of the speculative glances he cast in her direction, glances which for some unfathomable reason caused her an uncomfortable tingling of nerves. Her eye and face were healed and she was almost her usual self; it was owing to this that a mistrust of him set in, for it did seem that he was assessing her appearance and seeing whether or not it "came up to his requirements" as he had made the term, on suggesting she might become his pillow friend. In consequence of her mistrust the dressing-table had been moved on its silent castors and placed protectingly against her bedroom door each night; she would very much have liked to ask for a lock for the door, but knew instinctively that she would not be allowed to have one fixed. Besides, she thought, the very mention of a lock might give him ideas. . . .

He was speaking at last, just when she was beginning to wonder if he had absorbed what she had said about the difficulty of informing her foster-mother that the marriage had broken up.

"I shouldn't let it worry you. You'll not be telling her it's broken up – not for some time."

Kim stared, the calm and dignified air he adopted staggering her almost as much as the words themselves.

"What did you say?"

Impatiently he frowned.

"You heard me." Inflexibility there and no mistake. Kim paled slightly, but her calm remained unimpaired as yet.

"Perhaps," she invited softly, "you'd like to explain?"

Damon looked at her, sweeping her figure from

head to foot, acute distaste in his eyes. Clearly he was seeing her as a crook, a cheap and nasty little racketeer – and a not very smart one at that. Casually he took possession of a chair facing the wide low window, which was open to allow the scents from the garden to enter the lovely apartment. Cicadas whirred in the olive trees; a woman's dark immobile silhouette was visible on the distant hillside where a flock of goats grazed beneath the fierce Grecian sun.

Bringing her gaze from the scene of pastoral peace, Kim repeated her request and presently she heard her husband's voice say quietly,

"The day following our marriage I brought over a specialist from London to see my mother. He decided to operate as in his opinion she had a fifty-fifty chance. . . ." Damon paused as if to afford his wife an opportunity of preparing herself for what was to come next. More of her colour receded, but her composure was still retained. "The operation," he continued presently, "appears to have been successful."

Kim said slowly,

"Successful? Your mother will live?"

"That's right."

She shook her head, staring at him from where she stood, in the middle of the room, and feigning incomprehension.

"I'm glad – naturally, Mr. – I mean, Damon. But I fail to see how it affects me. . . ." She allowed her voice to drift away to silence as her husband began shaking his head.

"The obtuse affectation won't work, Kim. I've already learned that, rotten little crook though you are, you're also a woman of more than average intelligence. You know exactly what I'm conveying to you."

"I do not!" The involuntary exclamation was in itself an admission that she did know what he was conveying and she bit her lip in vexation at the slip. "I'm not remaining here after the end of the week," she cried, fists clenching. "You really expect me to? What sort of a life will it be – for you as well as me? You don't want me in your house, contaminating it! I've never heard anything so absurd as your suggestion that I remain here –"

"It was not a suggestion –"

"Don't let's make an issue of it! Order – threat – I don't give a damn what it was – I'm not taking any notice of it! We made a bargain; I've kept to my side of it and you'll keep to yours!"

To her astonishment this outburst was received without rancour or wrath. He seemed to be faintly contrite at going back on his word.

"I understand your feelings about this matter," he conceded, but despite his demeanour Kim was in no way deceived. His black eyes, hard as onyx, had in their depths that sort of inflexibility which nothing could break. "For the next six weeks at least Mother must be kept quiet; nothing must worry her in any way at all. A shock could kill her," he said significantly, "and I'm sure that even you would not wish that to happen."

Kim gritted her teeth, the "even you" having the effect of inflaming her. Undoubtedly she did not want his mother to die, but she would see this abominable creature in Hades before she would tell him so!

"You're crediting me with compassion? I'm amazed!"

His eyes kindled; he appeared to have come to the end of his patience.

"Cut out this air of injured innocence! It's beginning to pall. You seem to forget you're a crook, a would-be kidnapper!" He glowered at her across the room, equally inflamed as she now that he had reminded himself of the humiliation her had suffered at her hands. "You're staying here until my mother's recovered – fully recovered, get that!" His mouth was tightly drawn back from his teeth, almost in a snarl, she thought, fascinated by the dark blood that she could plainly see racing along a vein in his temple. She had never witnessed emotion like this and in spite of herself she felt a fluttering of trepidation. The man was dangerous ... highly dangerous, like an explosive. Nevertheless, she could not allow herself to be dominated in this way, and, her own face red with fury, she opened her mouth to retaliate. But anticipating her angry intention Damon forestalled her by reminding her that his threat of prosecution still stood. "You're in no position to argue," he ended, and his wife's green eyes glittered as her fury increased.

"You're a blackmailer!" she flung at him derisively. "And blackmail's a criminal offence."

One black brow slanted.

"I think the least said about criminal offences the better," he commented softly, and she gave a little gesture of exasperation.

"We're getting nowhere," she said. "Let's leave my crime out of it!"

"Why should we?"

Kim had no answer. She was struck by the sudden realization that her anger had abated within a matter of seconds and now her thoughts were concentrated on Damon's mother, whom she liked, and for whom she had felt the greatest compasion on seeing her in hospital, lying there, so brave, believing she was soon to die. Her life had been saved, but she was still in danger. A shock could kill her. This fact stood out,

76

occupying Kim's mind to the exclusion of all else.

At length, her decision made, she turned to her husband and for a moment his appearance held her whole attention. There was no doubt about it, the man possessed some outstandingly attractive features. The bronzed skin, the low noble forehead, the cleft chin. She noted the full lips and straight classical nose, both characteristic of the ancient Hellenes, pagans all. Her eyes fell to the white cuffs below light grey linen sleeves, to the gold wrist-watch band against a tawny wrist. He was watching her, arrogance in every line of him – arrogance and inflexibility. Superior creature! Full of self-assurance and conceit even now, when he should be just the opposite, depending as he was on her co-operation. His whole manner infuriated her and, some mischief entering into her, she resolved to keep secret her compassion and concern for the woman lying in hospital, and to allow Damon to believe that he had coerced her into remaining here as his wife. In this way surely he would suffer pangs of conscience, carrying the guilt resultant on the breaking of his word. He was a blackmailer, she would constantly remind him; his word meant nothing. Without a hearing he had branded her a criminal; she would now be able to call him a cheat. Yes, she thought, eyes kindling, just let him mention the expression "cheap little crook" again! She would have something with which to retaliate!

But for one undecided moment Kim hesitated, honesty uppermost in her mind. Damon was following his present course with exceeding reluctance; this much she freely owned. Instinctively she knew he was a man whose word would normally be his bond; in this instance he had to go back on it in order to save his mother's life, a course she herself would not have hesitated to take were she in his place. Another thing which struck her was that in any case he was trying a bluff, since she could not see him handing his wife over to the police. The girl, Kim Lyttleton, yes, perhaps, but not Mrs. Souris.

"If I were a nice girl," she told herself, "I'd be honest and admit that I was agreeing to remain here solely because of my concern for his mother – and because if I didn't have that concern, and insisted on leaving, I could never live with my conscience."

But the small urge for complete honesty dissolved as Damon, black eyes fixed upon her, seemed to frown in thought and with quick suspicion Kim felt he was wishing with all his heart that he did not have to harbour this criminal in his house. Her teeth snapped together.

"Seeing that I've no option," she said in stiff and choking accents, "I must remain here. But I hope you'll keep in mind just what you are – a cheat and a blackmailer." Contemptuously she raked him and to her intense satisfaction all he did was to glance away.

"You'll not lose by it," he said curtly, and Kim found it impossible to check the retort that rose to her lips.

"How do you know? My trade is exceedingly lucrative!"

Damon turned his head, and glowered at her. But he seemed to hold back what he had intended uttering and all he said was,

"Estimate your losses and I'll make them good."

She coloured, ashamed of her involuntary exclamation. And without another word she left him, and went to a small apartment whose view was on to the garden and orchard and the tranquil hills beyond. This was a beautiful island, she was thinking some minutes later, after managing to put the recent scene from her. Yes,

78

it was a beautiful island, and with her innate resilience she made a firm resolve to get all she could from her enforced sojourn on Cos. It had a great deal to offer and it was most unlikely that she would ever visit it again.

Her eyes wandered to another house farther down the hill; it was a rambling place which gave the impression of being occupied by an eccentric. Its walls were literally covered by climbing plants; it had pseudo Turkish arches and balconies with elaborately carved wooden rails. The garden appeared to be full of "follies" of various descriptions. There was a fountain, Kim had noticed one day as she passed, and she saw white stone steps which seemed to lead nowhere at all. There was a waterway over which were bridges of all shapes and sizes, some being made of wood while others were of stone. Colourful gnomes grinned at each other across its banks and bright green toads looked ready to take off at any moment and dive for food.

Into Kim's half-amused vision a tall dark figure intruded. Damon was walking in the garden; he stopped and, picking a rose, put the stem – to her great astonishment – between his teeth. She gave a small gasp, and a flash of memory brought back the strange sensation she had experienced on the yacht, when Damon had left her cabin. It was the sort of feeling never experienced by her on any previous occasion – a sensation half pleasant, half exciting in a sort of frightened kind of way. It had made her heartbeats quicken then, and it did the same now. A big man, with arrogance even in the way he held himself; a man of inordinate self-assurance, a man of strength ... and there he was, with a flower between his teeth. Kim's green eyes followed him; she recalled her impression that there was something contradictory about the man. She allowed her mind to wander, trying to imagine his feelings on having what he naturally believed was a gun pushed between his shoulder blades. Kim felt convinced that his first instinct would have been to stop the car, turn immediately, and tackle whoever it was sitting there behind him, but he had allowed caution to prevail. She could, now that she knew him better, imagine his gall and fury at his helplessness, could see him using his brain furiously, determined to extricate himself from this dire position in which he found himself. To submit meekly to being abducted must never for one single moment have crossed his mind, and Kim squirmed a little on recalling her own confidence and elation. She and her friends were clever, she had actually whispered to herself when, as she and Damon trod the narrow track, with the cottage in view, success seemed assured. Of course, had the whole thing not gone wrong from the start, and it had been Takis walking there in front of her, success most probably would have been assured.

Damon was now sitting on a stone seat by a small fountain, gazing into the spray which was transformed into a rainbow as the sun's bright rays filtered through it. Suddenly he took the rose from his mouth and tossed it angrily into the water beneath the fountain. But almost immediately he went to the side and with the aid of a small dead branch retrieved it, took a handkerchief from his pocket and dabbed it dry. Another gasp escaped her. What a strange, unfathomable man he was! A devil one moment and a child the next – a child with feelings and a sense of regret for an unkind action. Kim's nerves became oddly sensitized, she was conscious of a feeling of unrest creeping in upon her – a feeling she had known before. Tension, suspense and the subconscious desire for the unattainable ... these coalesced in her mind and clear thinking became difficult. She endeavoured to analyse her sensations, but failed. All she did know was that she was suddenly angry with the man down there, angry because he refused to accept her story, angry that, owing to his obstinacy, both he and she were unhappy. If only he would believe her at least they would not be fighting all the time. In fact, she thought, her nerves tingling again, they might even reach a state of friendliness because, the stigma having been removed, Damon would consider her his equal.

Kim lowered her eyes; they rested on her wedding ring. ... Something sharp touched her heart, like the point of a needle, inflicting exquisite pain – and something like reason touched her brain. Another prick, of warning this time, and sanity eclipsed the dream that had only just been born. What wild desires had entered into her unbidden? How could she want a husband she did not love? Ashamed and blushing, she turned from the window, and from the man down there ... Satan in a child's clothing – or was it the other way round?

But although she had turned away she failed to put him from her thoughts. What impulse had caused him to fling away the rose? Was he angry at being compelled to go back on his word? Kim nodded absently, sure that this was the reason for his action in tossing the rose into the water. He was a man of honour, that was proved, a man who was greatly troubled at having to break his word, even to her, a criminal in his eyes. She frowned heavily, angry with him again. If only he would accept her story, she would reciprocate by putting his conscience at rest, admitting that she would have stayed, even without his threats, simply because she could not allow his mother to undergo a shock which was liable to kill her.

Kim would very much have liked to live quite separately from her husband, and she pointed out that this was possible, owing to the size of the villa, but Damon instantly cut her short, saying that he was not having his servants gossiping outside.

"Yannis and Elphida are cousins of two of my mother's servants," he told her, "so it is not possible for us to live entirely apart."

"I see." She paused a moment. "Will your mother be staying here when she comes out of hospital – for a time, I mean?"

"I'm trying to persuade her to do so, but she refuses. It isn't the time for argument, so I have allowed the matter to drop."

Kim thought of her bedroom, not having any communication with that of Damon, but far too close for her comfort. It was next door, in fact, and as she had been into a room at the very end of the passage, and liked the furnishings and the view, she asked if she could occupy it. The request brought a hint of sardonic amusement to her husband's face and she went red.

"You're quite safe where you are," he assured her. "I've decided that a crook won't make a very desirable pillow friend – beautiful as you are, now that you've lost your bumps and bruises."

Crook. . . . Valiantly she attempted to stem the retort which rose instantly to her lips, but it escaped, driven out by fury.

"A blackmailer and a cheat would make an even more undesirable pillow friend!"

Damon's eyes smouldered; she had caught him on a raw spot, that was for sure.

"Say that again and by God you'll smart! You don't appear to appreciate your good fortune. Had it not been for my mother, and the position I'm in, I'd have meted out a punishment that would have had you screaming for mercy, I told you that in the beginning! Play safe, girl, for if you insult me again I'll not be responsible for my actions!"

Pale and with her heartbeats thudding uncomfortably, Kim decided not to make any further retaliation, although her fury was almost choking her. His threats. . . . Would he go to the lengths of carrying them out? She had been convinced that he would never inflict any real physical hurt upon her, she recalled, but, looking at that smouldering countenance now, she was not at all sure. His temper was unpredictable; he had the inherited traits of mastery, of superiority, which men from the East always assumed. He was unused to the disrespect which she had persistently shown him and she was under no illusions about the result had she been one of his own country-women.

"So I can't have the bedroom?" was all she said, and he immediately shook his head.

"I've assured you that you're quite safe where you are."

At the dinner-table that evening Kim said quietly, "Damon, can we talk amicably for a short while?"

Her phrasing evidently afforded him a measure of amusement, for a smile touched the firm outline of his mouth.

"For a short while? By all means."

"I was telling you how awkward it would be to tell my foster-mother of my marriage, and of its break-up –"

"But as it's not now going to break up – not in the

immediate future – you have no problem."

"I have the problem of the marriage itself. I've no idea how to tell her, yet I must communicate, for she'll be out of her mind with worry."

Her husband glanced oddly at her.

"Your concern seems genuine enough," he said, the hint of surprise in his tone having the instant effect of making her seethe. "But why haven't you already communicated with her?"

"Because, on considering it more carefully, in the knowledge that I would be free in a week, I decided there was no need to mention my marriage at all. I would have to explain my absence, of course, and the truth was the only feasible explanation. I meant to tell her of my – er – abduction, but then say I'd managed to escape –" She stopped on noticing his expression. A frown knit his brow; he was beginning to be puzzled, and that meant hope.

"Go on," he pressed quietly. "I'm interested."

Kim looked frankly into his eyes.

"Mumsie – my foster-mother – would have been upset, but as long as I was now safe there'd have been no need for her to worry."

"You know," remarked Damon after a thoughtful pause, "when first you mentioned this foster-mother I didn't believe she existed."

"You didn't believe anything I said," she couldn't help reminding him, but he merely flicked a hand, dismissing the matter as unimportant.

"She obviously does exist. Tell me about her." His dark gaze held hers for a long moment before he added, "Hadn't you any parents, that you had to be put into the care of a foster-mother?"

"They died within six months of each other when I was a small child. Mrs. Rowe, as she was then, was a

84

widow with one little girl. She took in foster-children to supplement her income. There were three of us from the home."

Damon made no immediate comment; his eyes probed into hers across the table. She wondered if he were beginning to doubt his first estimation of her character. There was nothing to be read from his expression and when he spoke his tones were curt and cool and edged with that faint accent which Kim had already found attractive.

"These others ... were they the accomplices you spoke of?"

Kim ground her teeth.

"They helped me, yes," she snapped, having no alternative other than to tell the truth.

"Mrs. Rowe evidently didn't make a very good job of your upbringing," he commented thoughtfully. "How very strange that all three of you turned out bad."

The green eyes lighted up.

"I asked if we might talk amicably!" she flashed. "Must you be forever goading me?"

Damon narrowed his gaze.

"Control yourself! I've never known a woman flare up the way you do. Practise a little self-restraint when you're in my presence."

Kim drew a deep and quivering breath. Her eyes lighted on an exquisite silver mustard pot and she debated for one inflamed second whether or not to pick it up and throw it at him, but she controlled the impulse and tried again.

"I'm endeavouring to tell you about Mumsie. I shall have to write to her, telling her of my marriage, now that I'm to live here for a while." Kim broke off and shook her head. "How I'm to convince her that

I'm happily married I don't know, but I must convince her."

"I expect," remarked Damon after a pause, "that, with your imaginative mind, you'll contrive something." He stopped as her mouth tightened. "I don't quite see," he continued when she failed to voice the retort he was expecting, "why you wish to talk to me about it?"

"Because, knowing my foster-mother, and taking into account the strange circumstances of my marriage, I would not be at all surprised were she to decide suddenly to come over here to see me. She's always wanted to know all about any situation in which we found ourselves, and as I said, the circumstances of my marriage were strange. She worries about us, you see, even though we've all left her now."

Damon was regarding her with the most odd expression. Clearly he was puzzled, but, unfortunately, not yet ready to accept her story, as his next words revealed.

"Can't you write a letter that will satisfy her?"

"I might, but she still could decide to come over, just to make quite sure that I'm happy."

A small pause, with Damon's face taking on an expression of sardonic amusement.

"I now see where I come in. I'm to take on the role of adoring husband. Nothing doing." Uncompromising the tones and Kim glared at him, blood surging into her cheeks.

"All right! But don't expect me to be your adoring wife when the time comes for your mother to see us together constantly! And what's more," she added, tapping the tablecloth with a furious finger, "I'm not coming to the hospital with you on Friday when your mother can receive two visitors at once –"

"You promised, and you'll keep that promise!"

"Never! You can't drag me to the hospital!" She did not mean a word of what she said, not really, but she was so infuriated by the one-sided business that all she wanted was for him to be filled with anxiety.

"All right," he said after a pause, "we'll call a truce when our respective parents are involved. When do you expect this Mrs. Rowe to come here?"

"I haven't even written to her yet. She might have to wait until her husband can come with her, I don't know. She isn't Mrs. Rowe now," added Kim quickly as Damon's eyebrows lifted in inquiry. "She married a Greek, and that's how she came to live in Athens."

Damon was eyeing her very curiously indeed now.

"She married a Greek, did she?"

"I mentioned this when I was telling you my story, on the yacht."

"You did? I wasn't taking much notice; the whole thing sounded so false that I took it for a complete fabrication of lies. However, part of it was true, it would appear."

All of it was true, she almost said, but resignedly pulled herself up. What was the use? The man was so stubborn that he was determined to retain his first impression of her.

"So am I to take it it will be all right for me to have my foster-mother here, if she does decide she wants to see me, that is?"

He nodded.

"But make sure she doesn't stop too long," he warned. "I'm not a patient man and a couple of days will be quite long enough for me to wear the role of loving husband." He paused, amused suddenly by the fire in her eyes. "What are you going to say to her?" he inquired curiously. "I expect the first thing you've to explain is why you've never mentioned me before?"

"If you won't listen to my story," she said with admirable control, "then please don't expect me to be able to explain, because it all connects up." And she just had to add, an acid edge of sarcasm to her voice, "as you so sapiently remarked, I'll contrive something, with my imaginative mind."

To her surprise he laughed.

"I like your sense of humour, Kim. Its bite lends flavour."

She inclined her head as if sarcastically acknowledging some grudgingly-extended praise.

"I'm happy to know there's at least one thing about me that you like!"

The black eyes flickered with amusement.

"More than one thing," he murmured, and she looked sharply at him, the piece of meat on the end of her fork suddenly poised in mid-air.

"More?" she echoed, angry that her voice was subdued. But she was reminded of his remarks about taking her for his pillow friend.

He read her thoughts with omniscient accuracy, and said in a heartless tone,

"Indeed yes. Your figure is delightful – about the most perfect I've seen, in fact."

"Oh . . .!" Colour flooded her cheeks. "You despicable creature! Have you no restraint – no sense of decency or respect?"

"Respect?" Damon's eyebrows rose. "Who would want to extend respect to a woman of your type?'

She said, voice quivering,

"You appear to have overlooked the fact that I'm your wife. I should imagine that, for the time being, you would have preferred to forget what I am. I expect you have friends on the island with whom I shall

88

inevitably come into contact, and these constant reminders that I'm a criminal might begin to weigh so heavily on me that I shall forget to be guarded when in company. I should hate to let you down by some slip of the tongue."

"What exactly do you mean by that?" he demanded, his eyes fixed on her face and noting her still heightened colour.

"We criminals have our own jargon, and – and that sort of thing. I might come out with expressions like swag and loot and several others I could mention," she ended rather triumphantly.

"Others?" he murmured, and she had the incredible impression that he was suppressing laughter. "Name a few?"

"You – you want to know some more?" He nodded, still watching her, his food forgotten. "Well ... there's filching and – and – er – I'm sure you don't want to hear any more."

"Oh, but I do. I'm extremely interested. Do please go on."

Kim eyed him suspiciously.

"You're laughing at me," she accused, filled with wonderment at the change in his expression. Gone was the satanic mien, and even the arrogance. He was amused, intrigued. He was enjoying himself at her expense and strangely she felt not a trace of resentment. Her anger had swiftly dissolved, much to her own amazement; her quivering nerves were back to normal, and she was now affected by a sense of excitement, vague, intangible, but hovering there, in her subconscious.

"Laughing?" His attention was returned to the food on his plate. "Tell me, Kim, just how long have you been at the game?"

"Game?" She blinked at him uncomprehendingly for a space and then, as she absorbed his meaning,

"Quite some time. As I said, it's a most lucrative trade."

He nodded, but absently. It was a meaningless gesture.

"I expect you've a large bank account?"

"Very large."

"How do you go on about income tax when you're in a game like that? I mean, the authorities must know about this accumulation of money."

Kim's eyes glittered. He glanced up at that moment and seemed fascinated by her expression. She had no idea how attractive she looked, in the pretty apple-green dress she had bought on the same day she had gone into Cos to buy her wedding clothes. Damon had been more than generous, because she had nothing except what she stood up in and therefore she required just about everything, from the skin up. That morning Kim had gone once again into Cos, to visit the hairdresser, and she had had a manicure at the same time. So she had turned up at the dinner-table looking exceedingly attractive – far different from the girl Damon had brought aboard his yacht so short a time ago.

"I'm sure," said Kim with cool reserve, "that you're not in the least interested in my private affairs. After all, they won't be troubling you a few weeks from now."

He merely shrugged; he seemed more interested in her expression than her words.

"You have eyes of the most extraordinary colour," he remarked at length. "They flash like green glass when you're angry." He was amused at the surprise she evinced. "And they flash quite often – but then you've the colour of hair that denotes a shrewish temper. I knew a woman once with ginger hair –"

"My hair," she cut in quiveringly, "is not ginger!"

"No? What colour is it, then?" She glared at him, but remained dumb. "No matter; it's still the colour that goes with the sort of temper you possess. I'd curb it for you were I sufficiently interested."

The green eyes glowed brighter than ever.

"You're so disgustingly sure of yourself! I dislike you intensely. Just how, might I ask, would you set about curbing my temper?"

An eyebrow slanted; the corner of Damon's mouth quivered slightly.

"I can think of several ways," he replied pleasantly. "The bucket of water could prove effective, I should imagine."

She went red, as he knew she would, and he looked at her hard and long, thoroughly enjoying her discomfiture. She felt deflated, and strangely lost for something to say. To her astonishment she realized she would have been happier if the conversation could have been more friendly.

"I – I d-don't believe you threw a bucket of water over me." Kim poked at the meat on her plate, then laid her fork down, her appetite gone all at once.

"Why?"

She blinked.

"Why?" she repeated.

"That's what I said. Why?"

She coughed to clear her throat.

"It wouldn't have been gentlemanly to do a thing like that – not when I was –" Abruptly she stopped, keeping her eyes lowered. Damon laughed – a most attractive laugh, and filled with humour.

"– stripped naked?" he finished, unsparing of her

blushes. "I assure you I did throw a bucket of water over you."

She swallowed.

"Then it was a callous, unmannerly thing to do to a helpless woman, who was unconscious and unable to defend herself."

"Defend? I wasn't intent on any form of mischief. You were the least attractive female I've ever clapped eyes on in my life."

"I didn't mean anything like –" Kim again pulled herself up. "You've already described the way I looked," she reminded him stiffly, deciding she must soon excuse herself and escape from a conversation that was becoming more and more embarrassing with each moment that passed, and all because Damon was deriving exceeding amusement from this embarrassment.

He said, having decided he had gone far enough,

"You were fully dressed when I threw the water over you."

She glanced up then.

"I was?" she breathed, unaware of the gratitude in her eyes. "Thank you for telling me."

"You're a strange girl, Kim," he said, his gaze searching and perplexed. "I asked you how long you'd been at the crime game. I rather think, now that I know you a little better, that you haven't had a great deal of experience."

His mood was more approachable. She said quietly, and with optimism,

"You're right, Damon, I haven't had a great deal of experience."

"What decided you to embark on that sort of career?"

"I explained everything to you on the yacht."

"That tale? You still persist in it?"

She sagged.

"You'll never believe it, will you?"

He shook his head.

"It's too absurd for belief. What about the gun?"

She hesitated a moment.

"If you remember, I said it wasn't a gun."

"Then what was it?" His eyes were narrowed; she sensed his rising anger and recalled her own conviction that he would far rather believe it was a gun that had forced him to obey those commands, rather than a small, harmless piece of wood. Should she tell him? Something warned Kim that she would only make a complete fool of herself, for he would never believe her, and in all honesty she could not blame him. As before she passed off his question without making any definite answer and as he himself did not pursue it Kim was left with the unhappy knowledge that despite Damon's more approachable mood, and her own optimism, she had not really made much headway as regards clearing herself in his eyes.

And, with a sort of stunning disbelief, she was forced to own that it had become of paramount importance that she clear herself in his eyes. . . .

CHAPTER SIX

KIM sat in the ancient agora, on a fallen white marble column, and enjoyed the silence and the sunshine and the deep awareness of being in the past. A high palm tree afforded her cool cover and looking from its shade she allowed her gaze to linger appreciatively on the beautiful ruins scattered all about the site, with wild gardens in between where bright reds and yellows and pinks shone up to the warm life-giving Grecian sun. Before her stood the Doric-columned portico with its triglyphs and metopes, and a solitary lion's head with its expressionless eyes staring down on the sad sight of fallen masonry that once had stood in awe-inspiring splendour, the pride of those who came here to worship in the temples dedicated to the gods of pagan Greece. A soft flutter of leaves in the breeze mingled with the chirping of cicadas and the gentle cooing of doves; a young couple strolled hand in hand along a path bordered by a bougainvillaea hedge, its brilliant crimson flowers lending even more variety and colour to the exotic scene.

Kim sighed contentedly. She loved antiquities and this island was a huge treasure chest of temples and shrines scattered over historical sites where many different civilizations could be traced. In the agora beautiful mosaics were left by the Romans; in the gymnasium were to be found remains of Roman highways, bath rooms and houses, but also there was the Gate of the Babtistere, a monument to the Christian era. In the caves were signs that the island had once been inhabited by the prehistoric Greek Pelasgeans. There was evidence of the Greek tribes from Asia Minor, of the Dorians and the Phoenicians. But of course it was the Italians who had to be thanked for the trees and flowers that adorned almost every road and street on the island. They had planted and planted, just as they had on Rhodes, and so Cos was a paradise of colour, a huge garden where the vista was one of exotic, breathtaking splendour. "A tiny piece of Paradise", it was called, and without doubt this was a perfect description.

"May I share your shady seat?"

Kim started visibly and looked up. The tall Englishman was smiling and already preparing to sit down.

"Of course." She moved, even though it was unnecessary; the column was long enough to seat half a dozen people.

"You don't recognize me, obviously." The cultured voice was tinged with amusement. "I'm your neighbour. I've seen you walking - quite alone. Naturally I'm curious. Damon Souris doesn't speak to me, so I couldn't question him about his guest. We had a bit of an argument once because I built a tower that marred his view. Obligingly I took it down, but it didn't mend our broken relationship. He considers me crazy. Do you?"

Kim wanted to laugh; she managed to keep a straight face, however, as she said,

"You're the man with the - er - unusual garden?"

"Don't be afraid to say what you really think. I'm the Folly man around these parts. You see, I'm distantly related to -" He stopped. "Perhaps I oughtn't to mention any names - although the poor man's dead now. I'm related to a titled Englishman who was inordinately fond of follies. He didn't know what to do with his great wealth and so be built all sorts of strange things. He had a place in Lancashire, if that's any clue?"

Again she had difficulty in repressing laughter. What an oddity: The Folly Man indeed!

"I know who you mean. I have lived in Lancashire. The Park is absurd in an attractive sort of way. There's something fascinating in climbing great stone steps that lead to nowhere, or crossing bridges that are quite unnecessary because there's nothing but the road underneath them."

"And nothing on either side of them, except the

parkland, of course. Mind if I smoke? It's foul-smelling tobacco."

Kim did laugh then.

"Carry on. You've no need to ask my permission." She felt she had known him for years! "Tell me about your follies."

"You've seen most of them. I haven't any idea why I build the wretched things; it's hereditary – in my blood. This blasted cousin of mine half a dozen times removed was crazy. Have you seen the barn he built?"

She nodded.

"I've danced in it."

"Half the population of London could be housed in it! What made him build a thing of those gigantic proportions?"

"I haven't any idea. There's another barn – smaller."

"I wonder what they cost him?"

"People like building. Bess of Hardwick was always building. We have her to thank for some lovely stately homes."

"Not Chatsworth now –" He wagged a forefinger at her. "That's what you're thinking about, isn't it?"

"No – not as it is today. I was thinking of Hardwick Hall and several others. But she did build Chatsworth originally." What was this conversation all about? Kim said, examining his tanned features and estimating his age at about thirty-five or a little more, "What was this tower you built and then demolished?"

He shrugged and frowned and absently stuck a singed thumb into the bowl of his pipe.

"It was to have been an observation tower."

"Yes? Er – what were you intending to observe?"

"The view."

96

"But you're on the hillside; you have an open view, like ours."

"It was a folly, remember. Follies are not meant to be sensible structures --" He stopped and laughed and prepared to strike a match. "If you get my meaning? What sort of a name do you have?"

Again she laughed, at his way of putting the question.

"Kim."

"Nice. Kim what?"

She hesitated a second or two.

"Kim Souris," she said, and watched his expression with interest. The deep-blue eyes widened and the long thick lashes went right back against his brows in consequence. Those eyes and lashes were wasted on a man, she thought.

"Souris . . .? Really?"

"Really."

He glanced at her wedding ring.

"Well, I'll be damned! An English girl! "

"Your name?" she queried after allowing him a moment's reflective thought as he lighted his pipe.

"Fergus Everard Zachary Smith."

"Smith! " she ejaculated before she could stop herself.

"I know," he sighed. "Even my name sounds like a folly."

"No – no, it doesn't." She looked apologetically at him. "I'm sorry for the exclamation. It was just that, with all those splendid forenames, I expected something rather more grand."

"Like Featherstonehaugh, for example?"

She burst out laughing.

"Tell me about yourself," she invited. "I haven't ever met anyone like you before."

97

"Nor will you again." He puffed and she choked. Foul . . .? It was noxious! "I lived in Cumberland, but the English take exception to follies such as I like to build and the neighbours complained to the local council. I wasn't popular, so I decided to live abroad. Here, one can do pretty much as one likes – unless one has a dictatorial neighbour like Damon Souris – Oh, the devil! I forgot. Sorry about that. How long have you been married?"

She told him and he nodded.

"I've seen you around about that long. You like it here?"

"It's a beautiful island."

"Becoming touristy, though, especially in Cos itself."

"The tourists don't trouble us; they keep to the places where entertainments can be found."

"True, true. Why are you here alone? You're still on your honeymoon – or should be."

"My husband has work to do."

"Really?" with a hint of scorn. "He's so filthy rich he has no need to work. Sorry again, dear girl. Don't heed my slips of the tongue. Wrong adjective."

"Are you married?" she inquired curiously, and one heavy shaggy eyebrow lifted.

"Now ask yourself – would any woman in her right senses marry a man like me?"

"Well. . . ."

"Don't bother about diplomacy. I'm an odd-bod who would drive a wife to suicide within a week."

Kim's laughter rang out over the quiet sunlit agora.

"Tell me what happened when you and Damon had words over the folly?"

"It was going up nicely – taller and taller and taller.

Well, I must admit that he got the devil of a shock when on returning from a trip to England he saw it. Damned unnerving, seeing an ugly great tower rising up to make a mess of your view. A hundred and forty-two steps there were already, and the blasted thing still growing –" He was brought up by Kim's laughter; she was almost doubled in two. "That's what happens when you build follies – they just get out of hand. Well, along comes your husband one evening, rage in his every step and murder in his eyes – Damned wicked eyes these Greeks have, but you must have noticed, being married to one. Yes, where was I?" He puffed at his pipe and a cloud of dark grey smoke billowed out, polluting the air all around. "I saw him coming and said to myself, here's trouble or I'll eat my hat! And it was – trouble with a vengeance!"

"And so you agreed to demolish your tower. That was obliging of you," she added politely, but secretly shuddering at the idea of a huge tower rising from the lovely tree-clad hillside.

"Obliging? I had no alternative. Oh, no, I didn't give in right away; perhaps our relationship wouldn't have suffered so much if I had. I told him I would do just what I liked. He threatened to blow it up."

"But he would never have dared do a thing like that."

"Perhaps not; he said it in a raging fury. I thought he would have done me an injury. However, he told me that it had to come down. He was powerful around these parts and what he said would go. I hadn't the strength to bother, so I gave orders for it to be pulled down. Your husband and I haven't spoken one word to each other since."

"Did you build something else in its place?"

"Of course. I built the Ark."

"The Ark? The barn we were talking about is called that."

"I know; mine's not a barn, nor is it that size. I might hold a dance in it some time, though. Will you come?"

"Without my husband?"

"He'll never come. No, I suppose you can't come without him."

She hesitated and then said she would think about it.

"My husband's often busy," she added. "I might be able to come without him." She looked curiously at him. "You have plenty of friends?"

"To come to the dance? I wouldn't call them friends, but you can always get people to come to a dance – especially when it's given by a curiosity like me. They have something to gossip about later." Another puff of evil smoke clouded the view. "How long are you staying here? Have you had your tea?"

"No; I thought of going to one of the *tavernas* for it."

"Want company?"

She hesitated, thinking of Damon. But then she decided it would be pleasant to have company. She felt like having another laugh or two

"Can you recommend anywhere?"

"I usually go to one of those on the waterfront. There's a very excellent café on Atki Kountourioti. Shall we go there?"

"All right." To her relief he knocked out his pipe and put it away in his pocket. "Is it far from here?"

"We could take a taxi – but we can walk if you like. It's a bit early for tea anyway."

They chatted as they strolled along; Kim could not

help liking the man regardless of the fact that he was most certainly an oddity. He talked about the island and she listened avidly, thirsting for knowledge that would not come her way once she had left Cos.

"You'll be getting bored by my chatter," he said as they sat under the shade of a bright canopy and ate sandwiches and drank tea.

"I won't; I love listening to people who are knowledgeable about places. Please go on."

"Very well." He paused a moment, cup poised close to his mouth. "Can I call you Kim?"

"Of course." She looked questioningly at him and he laughed. His bushy gold eyebrows looked most comical when he laughed; they seemed to sprout wings at the outer corners.

"You can choose," he told her obligingly in response to her unspoken question, "but I prefer Fergus."

She laughed and said she also preferred Fergus.

"You were telling me about Hercules coming to Cos," she then reminded him.

"It's all legend, of course. A raging storm shipwrecked him off these shores. He and his followers fought against the king, who was killed. Hercules married the king's widow and it was from their progeny that we get the great medicine man, Hippocrates."

"It's all so very interesting," she said enthusiastically when at last he suggested they make a move. "I could listen for ever."

"Then pop along to my place – Eridanos, it's called – and we'll have another chat."

"Eridanos?" she repeated, intrigued. "Why that name?"

"It popped out at me when I was reading a book on Greek mythology."

She laughed.

"What does it mean?"

"It was supposed to be a river; there isn't any other meaning, not that I know of."

Fergus came with her right to the gate, then said good-bye after thanking her for her delightful company.

"You'll be along tomorrow afternoon?" he reminded her as he turned to go.

Kim nodded her head.

"Yes, and thank you for inviting me."

"Pleasure. I hope the follies don't put you off for another time."

"I'm quite sure they won't," she assured him with a smile. He strode off, a tall angular man with a swinging gait. His long arms swung at his sides and his head was thrust slightly forward giving him a slightly humpbacked appearance. What a strange specimen of humanity!

So intrigued was she that she had to mention him to her husband that evening when they sat outside on the patio, Damon reading and she just staring contentedly at the dim outline of the mountain with its cover of lush vegetation, lit by the light from a full moon.

"Fergus Smith," repeated Damon with a frown. "Keep away from that maniac. He ought to be deported – would be if I had my way."

Kim's eyes twinkled.

"I enjoyed his company, as a matter of fact. Forgetting his peculiarities, you find him most interesting to talk to."

"And who," inquired Damon with a lift of his eyebrows, "could forget his peculiarities?"

"You're prejudiced. He told me about the tower."

"Such nonsense! The man's quite mad. Keep away

from him, I say."

"He's asked me over to his house tomorrow afternoon."

Damon laid his book down on the table, and leaned back in his chair.

"You say you got to know him when you were sightseeing? Are you in the habit of picking up with strange men?"

"Damon," she pleaded, having no wish to be troubled by her temper, "please don't goad me. I did not pick him up. He came and sat beside me in the agora, and he was so funny –"

"Funny peculiar, of course?"

"Funny ha ha! Have you no sense of humour? That tower, for instance – how could you fall out with him over it? I would have laughed for a week."

"You would? You didn't happen to see it."

"I meant, once he had agreed to demolish it. I thought it was the funniest thing – when he said, so seriously, that it kept on growing."

Damon became reflectively silent. And then, miraculously, his lips twitched.

"I suppose it was funny," he admitted after a while. "Although I couldn't see anything funny in it at the time. I saw red."

"I can imagine it," she returned drily. "He told me you threatened to blow it up."

"I would have done had he not had it demolished." Kim said nothing. She leant back comfortably in her chair and crossed her shapely legs one over the other. Damon's eyes wandered, slowly, taking in everything – and more than was on the surface, she thought with a swift and faintly apprehensive frown. Once or twice he had looked at her like this. She wished she dared ask for a lock or bolt to be fixed to her door. "You're not to go tomorrow," he said at last, and Kim gave a small start.

"What did you say, Damon?" Her chin lifted, and her eyes lit up.

"As you yourself reminded me, you are my wife. And my wife doesn't go off visiting men she has picked up in the street."

Silence. A hush that quivered with wrathful vibrations as Kim's cheeks reddened and her small fists clenched. But she valiantly crushed down the fury that was so rapidly rising up to fighting point, and she even managed to keep her voice low and steady.

"I'm going, Damon. I promised, and I see no reason for going back on my promise. There's no harm at all in my going to Fergus's house. He's the most harmless male I've ever come across."

"I said you were not going." Softly spoken words, but emphasised for all that. "I know what your argument is going to be," he said warningly as she opened her mouth, "but you can leave it unsaid."

Such cool dictatorship! Was he expecting her to stand for it?

"I can leave it unsaid, can I? Well, I'm not going to! There's nothing permanent about our marriage; there's no marriage at all really. And therefore I shall do just as I please."

From the hillside came drifting the lilting music of goat bells – so restful and pastoral and reminiscent of the simplicity of the peasant and his stock. This was no time for disunity, for indulging in quarrels. How she wished she could talk to her husband, asking him to believe her story . . . and to make friends with her.

"Kim," came the soft stern voice to violate her almost tender musings, "I think you know me sufficiently well to be sure that I shall make sure you obey me. My request is not unreasonable —"

"Request?"

"I expected that. I would prefer you to regard it as a request."

"But it is in effect a command?" Her tones were edged with a sort of acid sweetness which caused a dangerous gleam to enter his eyes. She looked into them by the light of the lanterns on the wall of the villa, and she was remembering Fergus's statement that Greeks have wicked eyes. It was quite true – at least with Damon. He had the most wicked eyes she had ever seen either in man or woman. They had great depth; they probed and pierced, and Kim knew that she had no chance of deceiving him – not in any way at all.

"I am certainly telling you not to go over to Smith's place tomorrow afternoon – nor any other afternoon, for that matter."

"And I'm telling you that I'm going over to his place – and shall do so just whenever I like."

He gave a small sigh; as yet no sign of anger was in evidence.

"We'll let the matter drop, Kim. I have a feeling you'll reconsider when you've given the matter a little quiet thought."

She opened her mouth, then closed it again. The argument could continue all evening. She had no wish for it to continue even while, paradoxically, she did want to convince him that she would do as she pleased.

He had picked up his book and after a few silent moments she got up and went for a stroll in the garden. Damon's mother was coming out of hospital in two days' time; she would stay at the villa for about a week and then she was going to her own home. She had plenty of people to look after her, she had insisted when Damon had made vigorous protests. In the end he had been forced to give in, as had he continued it would have had an adverse effect on Mrs. Souris's condition.

"I'll certainly stay for a week," she had agreed. "It will be nice seeing you together. What a dear girl Suzanne is."

"Mrs. Souris," said Kim when for a moment Damon had left them together, "I have another name – it's Kim. I prefer it, and would be glad if you could forget the Suzanne and call me Kim all the time?"

"But of course, my dear. Kim is very pretty indeed. Damon always called you Suzanne, you see. Will he call you Kim, do you think?"

"He already does, Mrs. Souris."

"Then why didn't he tell me? And, Kim dear, I'd like you to call me Mother."

Kim nodded. Damon had several times told her to do so, but she had felt too shy. Now, however, having asked her mother-in-law to call her Kim, she felt that it was incumbent on her to make the concession and address Mrs. Souris as Mother.

When on his return Damon had heard Kim addressed in her own name he had given a slight start, but immediately she had explained and he seemed glad she had had the idea of putting the name right. For he himself must surely have made a slip.

How would they all get along? wondered Kim as she strolled along the flagged path bordering the lawn. It would be a strain both for her and for Damon – especially Damon, she decided, because he held her in such high contempt.

As for herself – she could without the least effort have slipped into a friendly relationship with her husband, whose character she had been studying carefully this past day or so. Without a shadow of doubt he possessed a dual personality. The savage was inherent, a legacy from those dark days of paganism; the man who had held the rose between his teeth, and who could look so tenderly down into his mother's white face ... this was the man who was affecting her, profoundly. He was gentle, and he was kind. He worried about his mother; he would be overwhelmed with grief should her life now be cut short after all the hope and optimism brought about by the operation. She must not die – even though she had said she was ready to go. Kim surmised it had been her condition that had caused those words to be uttered. She had been so very ill, and in pain; she had been on the edge of the precipice, believing she was soon to be over the edge. It was understandable that she should have said she was ready to go. Kim hoped she would have many happy years left. The only thing which troubled Kim – and troubled her greatly – was the thought of the dreadful shock which the parting of her son and his wife was going to cause. That shock could not come yet, and in fact, after visiting her mother-in-law in hospital so many times as she had, Kim did wonder just how long a time must elapse before the separation could take place. And as she pondered on this Kim became more and more resigned to remaining at the villa for some considerable time to come.

And, strangely, the idea was acceptable, pleasantly so.

A soft footstep behind her and Kim turned her head; she stopped and Damon came up to her.

"It's a pleasant evening for a walk," he remarked conversationally. "The night air is always filled with such delightful scents."

Her pulses tingled in some delicious way. This was the man of today, not the pagan of the past. This was the man who affected her in a way she refused to analyse. And yet did she need to analyse . . .?

He was close; she felt the roughness of tweed against her arm, for he had donned a jacket. She inhaled the scent of something that in the shop would be labelled "His". Was it after-shave lotion, or hair cream? Could it be something akin to the feminine body lotion? She wished she knew more about a man's toilet. . . . Kim pushed these thoughts to one side, blushing in the dimness and feeling faintly ashamed — because her mind-pictures had gone just a little bit too far.

"Yes." Belatedly she replied to his remark. "I enjoy this particular time of the day. It's so deliciously cool after the heat of the afternoon. And as you say, the perfumes are — are — intoxicating."

She wondered if she was right in thinking that he smiled, or if she imagined it.

"I don't recall using that word."

"No. . . . Nevertheless, you'll agree that the scents are intoxicating?"

"I agree, yes," briefly and with a distinct tinge of humour. "You often walk out here at night?"

"I've done it ever since I came."

He strolled along beside her for a space and then,

"Have you heard from this Mumsie you talk about?"

"Not yet. I'm wondering if she's away from home. She and Petros might have gone off for a holiday somewhere." Kim had often wondered what had happened to Diana, but always she would put the distressing matter from her just as quickly as she could. Diana would probably have burned her boats soon after the

108

fiasco of the abduction, and as Kim could not bear to dwell on what this must have done to her foster-mother she shirked the pain of thinking too deeply about the matter. She would soon know what had happened because she was expecting replies to the letters she had sent to Enid and Pauline. She had sent them to their respective homes in England and by now they would have written back. How astonished they would be by her news – and how horrified.

"You've had no letters at all." Subtle the words, neither statement nor question, because he was uncertain as to whether or not she had received any letters, although he would be almost sure she had not for he was almost always there when the mail was delivered. On a couple of occasions it had arrived before he came from his room, and it was Kim who had put the letters on the hall table.

"I'm expecting some any day now."

"From your accomplices as well as your mother?"

She swallowed the anger rising in her throat.

"From Pauline and Enid, yes."

He seemed to be thinking about these two girls whom she had several times mentioned to him. After a while he said,

"Why don't you ask them out here for a holiday?"

Kim stopped in her tracks, so great was her surprise.

"My – my accomplices?" Never would she have thought to describe them herself in this way, but she just had to, in order to note the effect on her husband.

"You always maintain they were not your accomplices."

"I admitted they helped me."

"But you disliked intensely the term you yourself have just used."

"It isn't a nice term."

"Yet you used it," he persisted.

"Just to note your reaction. I mean," she went on to elucidate, "it was so odd – your offer to have them here."

He had stopped also and now he looked down into her face, examining it by the light of the moon. She knew she was flushed, that her eyes were bright – but not with temper. Her lips quivered and parted; she wondered if he were totally immune, insensible to the near-offer she was making. Thoughts such as these naturally had the effect of heightening her colour even more and she saw his eyes kindle ... and she caught her breath, frightened, because the present-day man did not have that expression in his eyes. No, that was the wicked expression mentioned by Fergus; this was the pagan, the man from the past.

"I understand." His words had no meaning since she had forgotten to what they apertained. She was trembling, and she knew not whether it was sheer undiluted fright that caused her trembling, or whether it was the less disturbing sense of expectancy mingled with a milder form of fear – that sort of fear which bordered on anticipation of the unknown. Did she want this man who in the first instance had treated her so disrespectfully – stripping her and then reminding her that there was nothing he had not seen – more than once? But she had long since forgiven him, admitting that he had an excuse for everything he did.

"If only he would accept my story," she whispered for the twentieth time at least.

"I'm sorry; I've forgotten what we were talking about." Kim began walking on again.

"I was saying you might like to invite your – sisters over for a holiday."

"Sisters ..." Kim's face broke into a smile and she

110

stopped again involuntarily and looked up at him. "Thank you, Damon." Her voice quivered; she asked herself with wonderment what she was about. She was playing with fire – but carefully. "They've just had a holiday – I did explain, but never mind that just now," she added hastily, fearing any mention of anything remotely relating to their escapade must surely put an abrupt end to this pleasant interlude in the otherwise antagonistic relationship existing between her husband and herself. "They couldn't get away until Christmas."

"So long as that?" She noticed he made no mention of the fact that she would be gone from Cos by that time, and Kim knew that he also had been thinking about the shock to his mother and deciding it must not come for a long while yet. "They couldn't have a few days in the autumn?"

"I don't think so. I could ask them." She was guarded, cautious. He wanted to see her sisters, to assess their character. Once he had done so then all would be well. They would relate the story she herself had related and surely he would then be willing to accept it. And afterwards. . . .

Kim turned with the intention of continuing her walk, but a hold on her wrist stopped her and she twisted round to face her husband. The touch sent vibrations through her entire body . . . and he knew of it. Swiftly she tried to escape, but he held on to her wrist.

"Kim," he murmured huskily, "my wife!"

"No!" She tugged in earnest. Yet another side of her backed him to win. What on earth had come over her? She could not succumb – not to this man who was a stranger still. Stranger . . . but no. Somehow, perhaps owing to their incessant quarrelling, she seemed to have known him for months at least. "I – I think

I'll be going in –"

"So do I." But she was in his arms, her lips tempting yet fighting, her body stiff yet ready any moment to yield. And it did yield, and so did her lips. It was heaven. He had practised the art and she had no will to resist. For a long time he kissed her eager lips, and caressed her gently. "Yes, my lovely wife, we'll go in!"

CHAPTER SEVEN

THEY walked slowly, neither speaking. Kim's feelings were mixed and even now she was not sure whether, once in the house, she would change her mind. That she wanted her husband she could not deny; that she cherished the idea that once she was his he would be bound to like her a little was also uppermost in her mind. But from a more realistic point of view she must own that it was desire and desire alone that occupied *his* mind at the moment, and she knew full well that marriages in Greece, being so often arranged, could run their full course without love ever entering into them at all. Love. . . . She was unable to assess for sure whether or not it was love she felt for her husband. All she did know was that she was content to be with him – when he was in a mellow mood, of course. And she also knew that the prospect of remaining at the villa indefinitely no longer troubled her in the least. In so short a time her feelings had undergone so great a change! At first she had counted the hours. Then had come the disappointment which she regarded in the light of a sacrifice on her part, having to postpone her departure owing to the operation which had saved his mother's life. Yet now she was content to remain. In fact, she would not even dwell for a moment on the idea of leaving.

She sent Damon a sideways glance. His profile was stern, his mouth unsmiling. What were his thoughts? She was his wife; in his opinion he had every right to claim her. Was this what he was thinking? The idea hurt and for a moment she knew the desire to stop and tell him that she had changed her mind. But somehow she felt too shy to bring up the subject. In fact, it was all too embarrassing, now that this stroll back to the house had interrupted their lovemaking. It seemed almost immoral to go calmly into a bedroom with the express intention of satisfying their desires. It was cheap and nasty, and she began to make up all sorts of excuses which she would put into words once they were in the house. But she had no opportunity for protests. Damon picked her up as soon as they reached the patio and carried her along to her bedroom. She was in his arms instantly he put her on her feet and it seemed there had been no interruption at all, so cleverly did he handle the situation.

She was part of him through a timeless interlude of ecstasy, and with the first shafts of light she woke and smiled and felt deliriously happy. Surely he could never make love like that without love! So tender and gentle, and yet so passionate. He stirred beside her but did not waken. She got up and took a shower; she was dressed and looking exceedingly pretty and happy when at last he opened his eyes and looked at her across the room.

"You're an early bird. Couldn't you sleep?"

She paled at his tone and the happy light faded from her eyes.

"It's past nine o'clock." Her voice was husky; she had a strange little ache in her throat. "I – I've only been up about half an hour."

Damon hitched himself on one elbow. His hair was tousled; he looked excitingly attractive, she thought, but still the ache remained.

"Past nine, is it? Well, what's the hurry? Come back to bed."

Her colour returned, flooding her entire face.

"Breakfast will be ready," she murmured, blinking rapidly to keep back the cloud of tears gathering in her eyes. So he had taken her as he would take a . . . pillow friend. There was nothing more to it than that. Any woman would have given him the same pleasure. What did he think of her? Cruelly his words about a "moll" came back to add to her torture. She lowered her eyes, wondering what he would say were she to tell him that she loved him. Oh, yes, there was no doubt in her mind now.

"Breakfast? Very well, my dear, I'll get up and we'll have breakfast together." Unemotional words and expression. His eyes had missed her quivering lips and the tears that escaped and hung on her lashes; he took it for granted that the experience had meant the same to her as it had to him. Bitterly she wished she could go back, but it was too late.

And she found also that Damon's intention was to keep the marriage on this new footing. She protested, but to no avail. She tried to resist and he scoffed at her; if she wanted a fight then it was all right with him, he said.

"I'm not living with you as your wife!" she had shot at him the very next night, but he had come to her room and his will had prevailed. The following night she could make no protest, as his mother's room was

114

opposite, and so Kim had been forced to keep her peace.

But Damon had said,

"What the devil's wrong with you? You enjoyed it the first time well enough! Cut out the frigid female act and take what's offered." He was angry, that was what it was, and he said dreadful things to her in consequence. But now and then he was the man who picked the rose and held it between his teeth . . . no, not the man, but the child. And she would look lovingly down at him as he lay on the pillow, so relaxed and with a faint smile warming those cold stern lips. And she would ache to kiss those closed eyes and to cradle the tousled head against her breast. But instead she would find hot bitter tears falling on to her cheeks and she would rise from the bed and leave him sleeping, because should he wake while she was there he would look at her with contempt in his eyes and his wandering glance would run insolently over her slender figure, and she would be left in no doubt whatsoever as to his thoughts and the way in which he regarded her.

Happily, though, Mrs. Souris made life pleasant, treating Kim with ever deepening affection.

"I must admit I didn't want him to marry a foreigner," she told Kim one day when they were both relaxing in a shady corner of the garden, Mrs. Souris on the luxurious garden bed her son had bought for her, and Kim on a less expensive but equally comfortable chair. "However, I'm glad now that he chose you. I always wanted a daughter, and now I have the most charming one imaginable –" She broke off as Kim blushed and then continued, "I keep telling Damon how lucky he is. I do hope he keeps what I say always in mind, for marriage is such a gamble and often it's the man's lack of understanding that causes hurt to his wife and, consequently, the falling off of affection on both sides. But he loves you dearly and I'm sure he always will."

Kim nodded dumbly. The tender attitude of her husband's was often like salt in a wound, more painful than his indifference would have been, since she was always acutely aware that his tenderness was merely for show, for the benefit of his mother, who must be deceived into believing that her son was happily married. Kim's own tenderness was very real, and often she would wonder how he could miss her sincerity. Perhaps it was because she still resisted to some extent his lovemaking. She was no pillow friend in her own eyes and she bitterly resented his treating her like one.

She had intended defying him over the visit to Fergus's home, but had given way, hoping her meek surrender would chalk up a mark in her favour, but Damon had arrogantly remarked,

"I'm glad you know what's good for you. You're married to a Greek, and if you're wise you'll keep in mind that the Greek husband is the master."

Retaliation had flared, but she had kept her temper in check. And now that his mother was living with them she had no opportunity of answering Damon back, even in the privacy of their bedroom, since she always raised her voice in anger – not like Damon, who could speak so softly – oh, so very softly! – but danger lay perilously close on many an occasion, and Kim was fast discovering that her husband was more to be feared when he spoke in this soft manner than when he raised his voice – which of course he never did these days, not with his mother being in the house.

Kim received two letters one morning and she saw

that Damon's interested gaze was upon her as she withdrew Pauline's letter from its envelope and began to read it. As she expected, Pauline was shocked at what had occurred. She wrote of the anxiety through which she and Enid had passed.

"We were almost out of our minds, Kim, waiting there and wondering what had happened. We had seen the car lights, then lost them, and knew you were in that part of the lane where the bend is. We naturally expected you both within about two minutes at the most, but three went by and then four. We decided to come and see what was happening. We saw the car backing rapidly down the lane and knew something awful had happened. In the light from the torch we saw your black beret floating on that filthy pond and you can imagine how we felt! Of course we knew you weren't in the pond, but we also suspected that you'd either fallen in it or been pushed. What we couldn't understand was where you had got to. At first we just couldn't believe the man would take you off in his car, so we searched and searched, thinking that you were staggering about in those woods, having been hit on the head or something.

"We stayed until daylight and kept on searching. Then we went to the police. It was awful; they wouldn't believe us. They seemed to think it was some sort of a stunt. Then there was Mumsie. Kim, you'll never know what we went through telling her. She also went to the police and she was believed. But you never turned up, and no wonder. Married! It sounds incredible."

More was written in the same vein and then, right at the end, Pauline dropped her bombshell. "And after all that, Diana had decided not to run off with this bloke after all. She told Mumsie that she'd decided he was too old for her and in any case she had recently met a nice boy and she thought she would go steady with him. What do you think of that? And you, poor thing, married to a man you don't even know. How did you feel on that yacht? I'd have been so terrified of the man that I'd have thrown myself overboard, for they're not to be trusted, those Greeks."

Kim was actually laughing softly to herself, forgetful for the moment of her husband sitting there, at the other side of the breakfast table.

"Death before dishonour," she murmured, in a whisper, but her husband caught it.

"What?"

"Nothing," she began hastily, but he interrupted her with,

"Death before dishonour? That sounds like something out of a drama – or a comedy. Who, might I ask, chooses death before dishonour, and why?"

There was nothing for it but to tell him the truth. For one moment Kim was tempted to pass the letter to him, and so clear herself, but she was so disillusioned by Damon's conduct in forcing her to be his light-o'-love, as it were, that she kept the letter from him. He could never care for her, that was evident, and so it no longer seemed important that she should bother to clear herself. She would remain on Cos until such time as it was safe to tell Mrs. Souris the truth, and then she would return to England.

"It's Pauline. She says she would have thrown herself overboard rather than risk – er. . . ." Kim fell silent, her colour rising. Damon laughed, greatly amused.

"Rather than risk losing her honour?" An eyebrow slanted. "Do western women have any honour these days?"

Pale and hurt, Kim said nothing, but returned to the letter.

Pauline went on to express more sympathy, asking if she could do anything to help, then immediately going on to admit that there was nothing.

"The wrong man —" It was the third time Pauline had written this and Kim had no difficulty in visualizing how her mind had run. Every now and then this must have come to the forefront and she had written it down. "The wrong man! It doesn't seem possible that such a coincidence could have occurred. Takis knew that Diana had changed her mind; she told us she had rung him earlier in the day, and so he wouldn't have been at the Imperial. But that silly fool had to be there — and in a Mercedes! Kim, I'd feel like killing him, just for being in that place at that particular time. What will you do — get a divorce, I suppose? You can't stay married to a man you don't know."

The letter ran to another couple of pages; Damon continued to watch his wife's face, noting its continually-changing expression. He was curious; she was again tempted to pass the letter over, but obstinacy prevailed. Let him go on believing she was a criminal. At least it made her own position less humiliating. Far better to let him go on thinking she had been a "moll" than allow him the satisfaction of knowing he had taken an innocent girl against her will . . . well, almost against her will, she amended, incurably honest, even with herself.

"May I read your letter?" The question was put quietly; Damon's open palm was already across the table as he waited to accept the letter from her. Carefully she folded it and returned it to its envelope. His hand closed, tightly, and for some indefinable reason she shuddered. A hand stole to her throat; she was recalling the strength of his fingers when he had threatened to strangle her. Now, as then, she swallowed, for there was a hurt which she found it impossible to remove.

"Its contents are private," was all she said, and although she had not finished her breakfast she excused herself and left the table, going up to her bedroom to read Enid's letter in private. It was on similar lines to that of Pauline, containing the same passages of shocked disbelief, the same angry sentences deploring Diana's conduct, the same disgust at the coincidence.

"Mumsie blamed herself. She was in a terrible state, saying they would find your mutilated body somewhere. She must have taken ill, I think, because her husband wrote and said he was taking her away for a holiday to Egypt. She didn't want to go, but he was making her. She must have been ill not to write herself, although I think she wrote to Pauline. However, you'll have written by now, so she'll know you're safe. What an end to that fiasco – you being forced into marriage. You say in your letter that you've assured Mumsie you're happily married. I'm glad, for that will keep her mind easy. I expect we'll see you soon, when you've got your freedom. How you must hate the imprisonment, because that's what it amounts to, isn't it?" More, like Pauline's letter.

Kim read to the end and laid it aside. Mumsie was in a terrible state, blaming herself. She had visualized her, Kim, murdered. Kim frowned heavily, aware that Pauline had omitted these details; she was more tactful than Enid, who let things slip, quite unintentionally. She didn't realize she was doing it. Kim's frown remained. It was her foster-mother of whom she was thinking. It hurt Kim that she should have suffered so much that she'd made herself ill. But it was to be expected, really, for she dearly loved the three girls – just as much as she loved her own daughter. Diana. ... Kim's temper flared as she thought about her – frightening her mother like that, and causing all the trouble. And then, after all that, she had thrown Takis over *before* Kim and the others had made the kidnapping bid.

"Before! Oh, I could wring her neck –" But Kim was shaking her head. She would never have met Damon, and even though she was immeasurably hurt and disillusioned, she could not honestly say she regretted having met him. What a strange thing love was! She would have been far better off had she never met Damon, since no heartache would have been hers, to carry for a long, long while into the lonely future, and yet she was glad she had known him, and cared. She was enriched by the experience of loving, and come what may, she could never lose what she had gained.

It was a week later that a letter arrived from Mumsie. It was the most wonderful letter Kim had ever received, or ever would receive. She had told her the marriage was happy and Mumsie had accepted this without question. But she wanted to know much more than Kim had told her in the letter, which she had received on returning from Egypt.

"It was like a miracle, for I never thought to see you alive again. And married to a charming and wealthy Greek. How glad I am, for I'm so happy in my own marriage that I know you will be too. Imagine being abducted, and then the gentleman falling in love with you and wanting you for his wife. It's so romantic that I'm sure Pauline and Enid must be envying you. And now, dear, when can we come over to see you? I must, Kim love, just to get the full picture. I can't come immediately, of course, because we've only just come back from a holiday – it wasn't a holiday, I can tell you, with that on my mind, but it's all over now and I can smile again. Well, Kim love, we'll come over just as soon as Petros can arrange to have more time off. He's just as eager as I to hear all about your adventure from your own lips. I expect the girls have answered your letters by now, as you say in yours to me that you were writing to them at the same time. They will have told you everything we went through so I won't bother to do so. You'll know that Diana changed her mind. She's now settled down with a charming boy from the American Embassy and I think they'll be getting engaged on her birthday as I heard them talking about a ring." There was a little more, and the end. Mumsie had, as always, ended with, "All my love, dearest Kim, and keep well. Mumsie." And three kisses. . . .

Kim's eyes glistened. She couldn't have loved a real mother any more than she loved Mumsie. What a darling she was! And as Kim had envisaged, she intended coming over to Cos. Well, Damon would then know the whole. But in the meantime he could go on believing her to be the cheap little crook he had on so many occasions called her. Not recently, it was true, and she surmised that this was owing to the fact of her being his wife. He had his pride and she suspected he thrust from his mind the fact that he had married so far beneath him.

Kim met Fergus again as she wandered down the lane one afternoon when Damon was working in his study and his mother was resting, as usual.

Fergus called to Kim from somewhere in his garden.

"Hi! Come on in. I've another folly to show you! "

Kim opened the gate and entered, scanning the area of shrubs from where the voice had come.

"Where are you?"

"Over here." He emerged from the shrubs, a spade in his hand. "I've just been digging in a totem pole."

"A what?"

"It's a hand-carved thing I saw in a shop in Athens the other day when I was over there. I couldn't resist it, because of the tremendous amount of work that's gone into it. Come and have a look. It's chickens."

"Chickens?" blinked Kim, bending to wriggle between the close-growing shrubs. "Did you say chickens?"

"That's right. I feel sure the man who carved it was a farmer – or at any rate, it was executed for a farmer. There are more chickens than anything else, but you'll find a cow and a pig and a couple of geese if you look carefully. But from about half way up it's nothing but chickens. Have you any theories as to why there are more chickens than anything else?"

Kim was speechless, her eyes beginning at the base of the totem pole and running up the full length of it.

"Fifteen feet?" she asked at last, dazed a little but on the borders of hysterical laughter. Fergus Everard Zachary Smith was without doubt quite mad – though harmlessly so.

"Oh, no, I shouldn't think so. Thirteen, maybe. The chickens – look, they're everywhere. All around it, and in all sorts of positions. Any theories?" he asked again.

"Perhaps," managed Kim, choking back her laughter, "he was a poultry farmer."

"Then why the cow and pig?"

"He'd keep those for milk and bacon."

Fergus snapped his fingers.

"Damned clever of you, Kim! Yes, of course that's the explanation. Do you like the blasted thing?"

"I don't know," with hesitancy. "What good is it?"

Impatiently he spread his hands.

"Follies never do any good! I thought of putting it in the middle of the lawn, but that blasted husband of your might just – Damn! Forgive me, Kim. Are you in love with him, by the way? I mean, it'll make things easier for me if you aren't."

"I'm newly married," she reminded him.

"What's that supposed to signify? Damon Souris is a Greek; they never marry for love. And he's rich; only reasonable to suspect you've married him for his money."

She couldn't be angry with him. It came as a shock to admit that had her husband said anything of the kind she would have flared instantly. But Fergus Everard Zachary Smith was so harmless, so inoffensive despite the content of his words.

"I assure you I didn't marry Damon for his money."

"For love?" He looked wonderingly at her.

"For love," she responded briefly. "Er – can we get out of here? I can hear the mosquitoes."

"They bother you?"

"Dreadfully."

"I'll give you some stuff to put on – before they bite you. Well, what I mean is, they won't bite you if you rub this cream on."

"Thank you. But if you give me the name of it I'll buy some myself."

"No, I'll give you the tube. I don't need it. The blasted things don't care for my kind of skin."

"That's better." Kim breathed again after emerging from the dimness of the shrubbery. "You can't see it in there."

"No. Well, as I said, I thought it would look just right in the middle of the lawn, but it would poke itself up into your husband's view – the one from his lounge. So I thought better of it. Can't keep having rows with one's neighbours. Now, what would you like to see? Pity you couldn't make it that day. Sorry to hear you had a headache." He paused and grinned and shook his head. The wings appeared at the ends of his bushy eyebrows. "Was it a headache – or Damon Souris? Damned dictatorial fellow! I thought he might forbid you to visit me. Did he?"

Kim nodded reluctantly.

"Yes, to be honest, he did."

"Damned petty! But these Greeks are like that. Don't know why I came to live with them."

"Cos is beautiful. You couldn't have chosen a more pleasant place to live."

"How do you know? Been anywhere else?"

"Well . . . no." Kim went slightly red.

"Still, you're probably right," a trifle absently as Fergus frowned at the spot in the centre of the lawn on which his eyes were focused. "It would have looked just right there. Perhaps I'll move it "

"Oh, I wouldn't if I were you," she cut in hastily. "It would, as you say, spoil our view."

He nodded resignedly.

"Come and look at the new bridge I've had made." He led the way. Kim was facinated by the way the stream – an artificial one – had been made to meander about the grounds. And every half a dozen yards or so was a bridge, each one quite enchantingly pretty in its own particular way. One was made of rustic poles, another of wrought-iron, another of stone and yet another of interwoven willow branches. Sitting by the bridges or along the banks of the stream were the frogs and gnomes and other creatures Kim had seen before. Toadstools abounded, of all sizes. Some were made of wood, others of stone; some were painted in bright blues and reds while others were left unadorned. What a conglomeration! And yet, taken individually, most of the absurdities of the garden were inoffensive. Some were decidedly attractive. "Like it?" Fergus stopped by his latest acquisition and stood admiring it. "Japanese design. They're marvellous at gardens. Ever been in a Japanese garden?"

"Not in Japan—"

"I know that, silly girl! I mean, in someone's stately home? They're always opening their gardens to the public. You must have been in one."

"Yes, I have." She mentioned it and he gave a short laugh. "Poor as church mice, that family. The old man married too many times — it was in the days when women could get alimony and breach of promise money — you won't remember because you weren't born. He married about five or six times — actresses, mainly, but I believe the last one was a barmaid. Got to open the house and grounds now — the son, of course; the old man's dead. So you liked the Japanese garden?"

She nodded.

"Yes, it was delightful. There were lots of bridges like this, over streams, and there were numerous waterfalls, I remember."

"I mean to have a few waterfalls some time. I'm just a bit worried in case your husband complains that his water supply's slow — the pressure's sure to drop, you see."

"It is? I thought you used the same water over and over again."

"You do, but it evaporates with the heat. You lose a lot – No, I don't think it's wise, not with a neighbour like Damon Souris."

"I must be going," she decided, glancing at her watch. "My mother-in-law will be expecting me to have tea with her."

"Yes?" Fergus fell into step beside Kim. "She's been very ill, I hear?"

"Very ill indeed. There was no hope for her; it was a tumour on the brain. But she had an operation and is recovering very nicely."

"I'm glad; only met her once, at a party which her nephew gave – name of Nico, I think. Nice fellow, not like your – And as I was saying, I liked Mrs. Souris. She chatted and we talked of the follies. She said that one should do what one desires to do and never mind anyone else. Mind you, I'd give anything to have been born without this blasted craze for follies. Yet I expect I should be grateful that I'm not as wealthy as you-know-who. He built such fantastic things. I do at least keep them reasonably small because I can't afford anything big – except the tower, of course. That was an extravagance and I'm not all that sorry I had to pull it down. The stone went into the making of several of these pretty bridges."

" 'Bye, Fergus," Kim was saying a few minutes later, "thank you very much for showing me around. I've thoroughly enjoyed it. I'll come again when I'm by this way."

"Please do. I'm almost always around somewhere. Just give me a shout."

"I will," she smiled, and stepped aside as he opened the gate for her. "I shouldn't move the totem pole," she advised, and Fergus laughed.

"I can take a hint. I'm not thinking of antagonizing

the wife as well. Good-bye, Kim, and thanks for your company."

She was thoughtful as she wandered back the way she had come. Fergus Smith was lonely. That was one of the reasons for all that clutter. It relieved the boredom to collect and scatter. He had variety in his grounds; he could wander among the absurdities and stand a while to ponder over one of them or admire another. An intelligent man, but lacking something.

"What he needs is a wife," decided Kim, and wished she knew of someone who might be suitable.

She mentioned this to her mother-in-law, who was in complete agreement.

"The poor nice man doesn't know what to do with himself. Oh, I know of this inherited trait for follies – most peculiar it is. From what he told me I gathered that one of his relatives had the same kink. Fergus says he's inherited it from him."

Kim mentioned the place in Lancashire where the follies were.

"The Park's public now," she went on, "and the children love it."

"I expect they do. But to get back to Fergus –"

"And who should want to get back to Fergus?" They both glanced up as Damon spoke. He didn't usually join Kim and his mother for tea, but evidently he intended doing so today, because one of the maids, Julia, was coming across the lawn with more crockery and sandwiches on a tray. Damon told her to bring a chair and this she did. He sat down, his eyes fixed on his wife's face interrogatingly. "Well?" softly as she remained silent. His mother answered,

"We were just saying that he needs a wife. Don't you agree, Damon?"

"A wife?" Damon stared at her. "Good God,

who'd marry an idiot like that?"

"The poor man's lonely. Kim agrees with me. She's been keeping him company this afternoon and she's seen all his ornaments and bridges and things. He needs something more interesting to do."

"Kim's been keeping him company, has she?" he said softly, eyes narrowed and glinting.

"That's right. He's just bought a totem pole –"

"A totem pole?" echoed Damon incredulously. "What in the name of Hades does anyone want with a totem pole?"

"It's another folly," put in Kim, angry with herself for the trepidation she was experiencing because of the manner in which her husband was looking at her. "It's very attractive, as a matter of fact. It's exquisitely carved."

"It is?" with a quality of disbelief. "How long have *you* been interested in the aesthetic?" His sarcasm was plain.

She coloured. But her eyes flitted to her mother-in-law, who was naturally looking with exceeding surprise at her son. The swift realization of what he had done resulted in a change of expression. Affectionately he smiled at his wife, whose own smile fluttered in response – but her green eyes were alive and she was quite ready for him when, later, he tackled her about her visit to Fergus's home.

"I shall please myself what I do! I'm not your slave! Don't come to the conclusion that this business is all one-sided, and that you can treat me just as you like. If you're not careful I shall retaliate! I'm acting a part, but it doesn't say I shall never get tired of acting. And," she added as a parting shot, because she was so inflamed with fury, "just remember what *you* are – a cheat and a blackmailer!" She stepped back

129

even as she spoke, for danger leapt into those wicked dark eyes. "You've no right to try and dictate to me," she faltered after a long and awful silence.

Damon continued to stare silently at her. She felt her colour fade and there was a nasty thudding in the region of her heart. How came she to fall in love with such a man? Life with him would be one long spell of fear.

"If you dare to mention the words cheat and black-mailer once more," he said softly at last, "I'll let you feel the strength of my fingers round your throat again."

"You – you consider me a cr-criminal –" She broke off, speech being difficult. It was ridiculous to feel the strength of my fingers round your throat in the house. And yet she was afraid, because of those eyes and that mouth and the way his jaw had become taut. His hands at his sides opened slowly and closed, a little rush of blood caused a vein in his temple to pulsate. "I'm doing no harm in going to see Fergus," she managed, determined to rally, if only feebly. "He's lonely, as I said, and although he's always cheerful I'm sure he isn't happy. If I can give him a little pleasure –"

"Pleasure?" he intervened with gentle insinuation. "In what way, might I ask?"

"You're hateful!" was all she could find to say, and she turned her back on him. She was swung round as his hands gripped her shoulders.

"Keep away from him, understand – Don't interrupt! By God, girl, I'll make you sting before I've finished with you! I said keep away, and I meant it!"

She moistened her lips.

"Can you give me a reason?" she managed to ask in spite of the blockage in her throat.

"I could give you one, a very excellent one, but I shan't." He released her, but tilted her face up with a rough hand under her chin. The firmness and arrogance in his touch sent fury surging through her – and yet she dared not knock away his hand, as she would so very much have liked to do. "Keep away," he advised softly again, "or you'll be feeling sorry for yourself . . . for a very long time."

CHAPTER EIGHT

IT was most odd, thought Kim with a frown as she strolled around the impressive ruins of the Asclepion, that no matter how she threatened she could not put any fear into Damon. It was as if he was confident that she would never do anything that would hurt his mother. Surely, then, this meant that he regarded her in a less contemptuous light than previously. If he believed she would always consider his mother's health and peace of mind then how could he continue to believe she was a hardened criminal? Perhaps hardened was an exaggeration; Damon had in one of his softer moods suggested she had not been at the "game" very long. Still, he did regard her as a criminal, which was at variance with the conviction he seemed to have that she would not carry out her threat to discontinue her act. That he had been curious for a spell was evident, and Kim now wondered if she had made a mistake in refusing to show her foster-sister's letter to him.

She thrust the whole wearisome business from her and set out to enjoy her visit to the Asclepion of Cos, where the greatest of all physicians of antiquity, Hip-

pocrates, taught and practised after building his wonderful hospital.

A Greek guide approached her and she smilingly
accepted his help. They strolled about together in the
sun, joined after a while by a group of American tourists, good-humoured, talkative, the women gaily but
casually dressed. Kim enjoyed the company and the
chatter; she found herself in conversation with a girl
of about her own age whose parents were also with the
party.

"We're at the Alexandra," she told Kim, who had
politely inquired if the party had come in to the island
from one of the cruise ships which were constantly cal-
ling at Cos. "We're here for a week and then we go on
to Rhodes. You . . .? Are you on holiday?"

"No, I live here."

"You do? Lucky! You have a job of some kind?"

"I'm married to a Greek," said Kim quietly, one
ear alert to hear what the guide was saying.

"– built on three platforms, and you will see the
beautiful wide magnificent staircase up which we will
proceed to get to the next platform. Follow me,
please!"

"Married to a Greek!" The American girl's voice
mingled with that of the guide. "How exciting. I'd love
to marry a Greek – so amorous! It's said they're the
greatest lovers in the world. Would you agree?"

Kim had to laugh.

"As I haven't had any other lovers I'm not in a position to agree or disagree."

Her companion responded to her laughter.

"No, I see what you mean." She and Kim tagged
along at the rear of the group. The guide stopped and
beckoned to them to hurry.

"First you will see the beautiful view from this top

platform –" He swept a hand towards the magnificent vista spreading out below them. "Hippocrates, you will see, chose the most wonderful place in all Cos. He believed in beauty as a medicine. This wood is the sacred forest of the sun-god Apollo. . . ." The guide went on and on, untiring, beckoning those who lagged behind, patiently waiting for them before beginning once again to explain the intricacies of the ancient archaeological site which dated back to the fourth century before Christ.

"Why," asked someone, "is it called the Asclepion?"

"All the temples dedicated to the god of medicine, Asclepius, were called Asclepions. In Greece we have about three hundred of these Asclepions."

"But you call the whole of this site the Asclepion?"

"That is correct, madam. The sites have taken the names of the temples."

"And Hippocrates was of course a human, not a pagan god."

"A human, of course, as you say, madam. He followed in the footsteps of the great god, building this hospital, but naturally building temples to Asclepius and his father, Apollo."

"I get all mixed up with the gods and the humans," a voice complained. "It all seems such a muddle."

"There are books, madam," pointed out the guide coldly. "It is possible to read it all up, if one is interested in Greek mythology."

"You said that Hippocrates, who was human, was descended from Asclepius. How could that be?"

"The gods sometimes married humans, madam. It is all in the books."

"Married humans? But the gods weren't really there – only in stone, I mean."

The guide shrugged his broad shoulders and repeated that it was all in the books.

"She's right," asserted Kim's companion, "you can't help getting all mixed up."

"It's a deep subject, but I'm becoming interested in it myself since coming to live here."

"What actual good does it do you, though? It's not like acquiring knowledge about science, or politics, for instance."

Kim smiled and said,

"I'm not particularly interested in either of those things. They're both destructive."

"And constructive."

"I can see only the destruction, and as it depresses me I avoid becoming interested. I like fairy tales," she added unashamedly.

"I'm a realist, I'm afraid; I expect I derive a lot less from life than you do."

Kim was silent, listening to the guide. A lot less. . . . A sigh escaped her. What a lot more *she* could get from life if only her husband could care for her a little.

"If you can imagine, ladies and gentlemen, all the gleaming white marble statues and temples standing on this tableland, which was cleared from the heart of the sacred forest, around which was a wall for protection. There were many little tumbling streams and waterfalls, and birds and flowers; it was very beautiful, as you can imagine." He spread a hand. "Today we have many flowers and trees, yes. It is because when the Italians were in occupation of our island they planted a great many trees here, and flowers also; they did the restoration and you will still notice some new marble columns lying about. These were for more restorations, but the island came back to Greece and the work was never finished."

At last the tour of the site was ended and Kim took a taxi into the town of Cos, where she had her lunch and then took another taxi home. Her mother-in-law had left a couple of days previously and Kim and her husband once more had the house to themselves. Kim and he had visited his mother the evening before and Kim had been enchanted with her small but luxuriously-furnished villa. It stood amid lovely gardens and the view to the mountains was magnificent. Nico and his sister were also there, and great was their interest and curiosity. They had not been invited to the wedding and as in Greece all the relations are invariably brought together on such occasions as weddings and christenings these two naturally evinced rather more than ordinary interest in their newly-acquired cousin-in-law.

Kim had carried off the difficult situation very well; she was aware at once that both these cousins of Damon's had been warned by him, since they were most guarded in all they said. On introducing his wife to Katrina he said,

"You've heard of her as Suzanne, but she prefers to be called by her other name, which is Kim."

"You might have thanked me," Kim flashed at her husband when, the visit over, she and he had driven away from the villa in his car. "I think I did very well indeed for you." She was piqued by his calm acceptance of all she had done; not once had he sent her a glance of appreciation for her efforts. "I could have let you down, you know."

"To your cost, it would have been." Damon increased his speed on reaching a long straight stretch of road.

"You couldn't show gratitude if you tried!"

"Don't let's have more of your tantrums. I threatened once to tackle that temper of yours! Watch yourself or I might decide to carry out my threat."

Kim dwelt on that homeward journey as she sat in the taxi after her pleasant tour of the Asclepion. Damon had had the last word, as always, and she was left quietly seething, wishing with all her heart she had the physical strength to repulse him, later, when he so arrogantly entered her bedroom. Always he wore the air of the conqueror, the man with rights, rights which he meant to assert. That he considered her in the light of a convenience was plain; he neither spoke of love nor looked at her with the sort of expression for which she so profoundly yearned. He was totally indifferent to her as a person. She was his wife and yet only his pillow friend. The humiliation was increasing all the time and Kim knew she was coming to the end of her endurance. Loving without love was not for her; she resented giving without receiving. Damon must make the most of his opportunities, she had been driven to warning him, for the moment his mother was able to stand the shock of a broken marriage she, Kim, would be off – back to Athens and then on to England.

She was to repeat the warning later when, having slid from the taxi, she came face to face with her husband as he emerged from the living-room on to the patio. She stood below and looked up at him, a ready smile trembling on her lips as she searched for some sign that he was in one of his mellow moods. His face was set.

"Where have you been?" he demanded imperiously.

"To the Asclepion." Kim began to mount the steps, but paused half way.

"Alone?"

"Of course. How could I go with anyone else?"

His eyes roved over her with what seemed very much like insolence in their dark depths. Kim valiantly controlled the anger that threatened.

"Our neighbour," he murmured, and her eyes did then take on their brittle illumination.

"And if I had been with Fergus – what of it! "

"Thank your stars you haven't been with him." Damon stepped aside as she covered the last couple of steps to the patio.

"You're just asking for me to defy you," she warned, brushing past him and standing by the open french door leading into the living-room. "Your aversion to him is ridiculous; the man's perfectly harmless."

At that Damon opened his mouth, but then closed it again. What had he been about to say? Something unnecessarily cutting, she decided, and went into the house. But he followed, and it was then that she repeated her warning that he make the most of his opportunities, as she was more than ready to leave his house.

His dark eyes kindled. He said quietly,

"You seem to forget that I have the whip hand."

"I can scarcely forget that you're blackmailing me –" She stopped, taking an urgent step backwards, but Damon was incensed by this repetition of what he had more than once warned her not to repeat. He almost leapt at her and she cried out as his grip savaged her shoulders.

"I told you not to use that word again! I'll –" His voice came to an abrupt halt. Turning, Kim stared at the girl standing there, a slim girl with blonde hair and big blue eyes. She wore a smart suit and a jaunty little hat with a bow of flowers and a tiny ruching of velvet cutting the brim in two. She carried a small suitcase and a leather handbag which matched her shoes.

"Suzanne! " Damon's grip on his wife's shoulders

137

slackened, then his hands fell to his sides. "Where the dickens have you come from?" His glance went automatically to the window. She had come by taxi, the girl said. She had left it at the gate and walked the length of the drive.

"I paid him off," she added, her eyes fixed on Kim, whose face was white and whose hands were clasped nervously together. "Did I arrive at an awkward time?" The voice was soft and purring, like a kitten when it's being petted.

Damon frowned darkly. Kim wanted to laugh — a trifle hysterically, it was true, since she was trembling inside from the expectation of being shaken by her irate husband. The situation was very funny, though. Kim knew a spiteful satisfaction at her husband's discomfort. But he soon recovered, as was to be expected. Damon Souris was not the man to be put out for long.

"Why didn't you let me know you were coming?" He held out a hand for the hat she had taken off. Fascinated, Kim watched this changed man — this polite and suave charmer who, having received the hat, waited while Suzanne unbuttoned the front of her jacket, then pushed forward a chair for her.

"I thought to surprise you."

"You've succeeded," tersely as he laid down the hat on the back of the settee. "Meet my wife. Kim, Suzanne, as you already know."

"Your wife?" The girl's face paled; she was as white as Kim. "You can't be married, Damon. You haven't had time!"

"I'll leave you," offered Kim, and went from the room.

"You can't be married!" Suzanne was repeating as Kim closed the door. "Oh, darling, you wouldn't have done that to me —!"

Kim stood outside the closed door, aware of a dampness on her forehead. The girl was lovely – slender as a nymph and attractive in every other way. Damon had been in love with her. . . . Or had he? Kim recalled her impression that he had not been too troubled by the broken engagement. Yet Suzanne was not the kind of girl whose charms could be ignored. If Damon had gone so far as to become engaged to her then surely he must have felt something for her.

What was happening in there? A reunion . . . intimate and emotional? Were they even now in each other's arms? Mouth quivering, Kim closed her eyes tightly. Courage she possessed in plenty, but this situation was crushing her. Jealousy was present, naturally, even though she knew she wanted to get away from her husband. But to leave and know he was alone was far different from leaving another woman in possession. Her chin lifted and her eyes sparkled. Suppose she decided not to leave? Damon could not throw her out. The next moment her head sank and her shoulders sagged. Damon was not hers; he never had been hers and he never would be. If any woman had a claim on him it must be Suzanne.

Kim's attention was suddenly caught by Fergus walking slowly along the lane in the direction of his villa, she determinedly threw off her dejection and left the house by the side door, so as to escape being seen by her husband or his companion. She caught Fergus up just as he was entering his drive.

"Hello," she greeted him a little breathlessly. "I saw you walking and thought I'd come along and have a chat." Company, that was what she desired – company and conversation, in order to prevent herself from dwelling on the scene over there . . . the reconciliation . . . the happy making up after Damon had explained that his marriage was necessary but that it was by no means permanent.

"Fine. I'm ready for one, I can tell you. Not spoken to a soul all day."

"I've been up to the Asclepion," she said, falling into step beside him as he walked slowly along his drive. "It was wonderful!"

"I thought so too. Only been once; must go again. We could go together if you like?"

"All right. But not yet awhile. Leave it another fortnight or so."

He glanced sideways at her; the bushy eyebrows fascinated her. She wanted to take a pair of scissors and trim them – drastically! She said, willing her mind to stop bringing Damon and Suzanne into her vision,

"Have you acquired anything new?"

"Since the totem pole? No." They had reached the patio, vine-shaded like that of Damon's. "Some tea?" he asked, and she nodded at once. "Take a seat then, I'll go and get it ready."

"You haven't a servant?"

"Can't be humbugged with the blighters. Unless you can pay a high wage you don't get the service. Your husband's the money to pay and it's his kind that send up the wages." He went off and she had to smile in spite of her deep dejection. If Fergus spent less on follies then he too could afford a servant. He returned with the tea in an incredibly short space of time. He always cut himself a huge pile of sandwiches first thing in the morning, he explained on noticing her surprise.

"I then haven't anything to do for the rest of the day." He put down the tray and began to pour the tea.

"You live on sandwiches only?"

"Nothing wrong in them, my dear. Sugar?"

"One, please."

"Not worried about your figure, then?"

"Not yet." Suzanne had a marvellous figure.... "Later, maybe."

"Later for sure. Middle-aged spread. None of us can avoid it. There you are, Kim. Help yourself to sandwiches – cheese here and salmon on that side. Tomorrow it'll be beef and eggs – just in case you think of coming over again." He sat down on the other side of the table. "How is it you're always alone? I never see your husband with you – except in the garden now and then. I have a good view from my back porch, you know. Can't see your front lawn, though, so if you're in the habit of sunbathing in the near-nothing don't be alarmed. How's Mrs. Souris? I heard she had gone back to her own place."

"She's improving wonderfully, thank you." She wondered from what source he heard things, but refrained from putting what she considered to be a pertinent and unnecessary question. She had no interest in the method by which he came by the local gossip.

"Miracle. I expect your husband's happy at the unexpected turn of events. He thinks the world of his mother – but these Greeks do – much more than their wives – here I go again! But you know me by now, I hope?"

She managed a thin smile. Was everything right now between Damon and Suzanne?

"Yes, Fergus, I understand you."

The wings fluttered at the ends of his eyebrows, as they always did when he laughed.

"I like you no end. Tell me, Kim, how are you liking married life?"

She stared, the question being totally unexpected.

"It's fine." How long would it last? Perhaps Damon and Suzanne were discussing the possibility of making a full confession to his mother and thereby making the way clear for their coming together more quickly than would otherwise have been possible. But no; Damon would take no risks where his mother was concerned.

"You're not over-enthusiastic," commented Fergus, watching her changing expression. "What are you thinking about?"

"Nothing – nothing important." She put down the sandwich and leant back in her chair. Were Damon and Suzanne taking afternoon tea together, in intimate seclusion, on the patio or terrace? Were they sitting like this, opposite to one another or close together?

Fergus seemed to be troubled by her expression and after a small silence he said gently,

"I'm a good listener, Kim. And I can keep my own counsel."

"What do you mean?"

"All right. Keep it to yourself. More tea? And what about that sandwich? Something wrong with it?"

"You know there isn't." Leaning forward, she picked it up.

"I'm troubled about you, Kim. I know we've only just recently got acquainted, but we're friends, aren't we?"

"Of course," with another weak smile.

"You're unhappy about something?"

She glanced swiftly at him, suddenly sensing that he had seen Suzanne's arrival at the villa.

"It's nothing, Fergus. Thank you for being troubled about me, though."

"It's *something*," he argued. A long pause and then, "Another woman? These Greeks ought to have harems – I know, because I've lived here long enough

142

to know their habits. Husbands don't remain faithful for long."

She hesitated. His eyes were wide and frank and kindly. She wanted all at once to confide, because she felt it would relieve the dreadful ache within her – the fear and the uncertainty.

Fergus listened, his expression strangely fixed. She experienced a small access of disappointment that he should not be portraying any sympathy either by the odd insertion into her narrative or by a change in his expression. She began to falter, already filled with regret at this confidence. She would never have made it had she not been feeling so low in spirits, or had she not known she would be leaving here in the not so distant future.

"And that's the whole story," she ended at last, taking up her cup and drinking deeply.

"And a most extraordinary story it is," he commented thoughtfully, his big blue eyes fixed on her face. "You were a brave young woman to try to kidnap a full-grown man."

"I had my sisters to help," she reminded him. Fears were rising; she would have given anything to put back the clock five minutes or so.

"Nevertheless it was a courageous action."

As Kim's one desire was now to prevent any questioning on his part she glanced at her watch and said it was time she was leaving.

"You haven't been here very long, my dear. Must you go so soon?"

She prepared to rise.

"Yes, I must, Fergus. I'll come again."

"Do, Kim." He stood up. "I'll walk to the gate with you."

She was still glad of his company, but uppermost in

143

her mind was the confidence she had made, and the regret she felt, which was most troublesome. She could not understand why it should be so troublesome; it was almost as if she feared her indiscretion would get back to Damon – which was an absurd notion since Fergus and he never spoke and, in any case, she was sure she could trust Fergus to respect her confidence and keep to himself what she had revealed.

Her footsteps flagged long before she reached the gate. But she would have to go in; there was nothing else for it. And she was heading for her bedroom when Damon came from the room which she knew was his study although she had never been inside it.

He looked at her face and subconsciously she averted her head, fearful of his reading guilt there or some other quality which would set him thinking.

"Where have you been?" he inquired softly.

"Oh, just for a walk," with forced lightness. "I felt that you and your fiancée would wish to be alone." She half expected him to deny having a fiancée, but was disappointed.

"How far did you walk?"

"How far? Er – right to the end of the lane."

"Yes? And then?"

She flashed him a glance.

"Does it matter?"

"I would like to know just how far you walked," he responded pleasantly, and she endeavoured to read him, suspicious of that tone. Basically she was honest and she hated lies, but there seemed to be a great need for dishonesty at this moment.

"I – I carried on, cutting across the field, and – and then wandered about for a little while. Then I came back."

The dark eyes were inscrutable.

"That's the truth?"

Kim's nerves tingled. She felt she had got herself entangled in a net that was gradually being tightened.

"Yes," she managed at length, "of course it's the truth."

He gave her a strange glance – a frightening glance.

"Come with me," he invited in that same pleasant tone.

"Wh – where to?" She thought of Suzanne and wondered where she was.

"Just to my study."

She went with him; he closed the door and she jumped as the latch clicked.

"Over there . . . by the window."

Bewilderedly she looked up into his dark set countenance. Why was he acting so strangely – and so frighteningly?

"Why the window?" But she found herself moving towards it and she was acutely aware that he followed closely.

"Take a look out," he invited, and now there was a pronounced change in his voice and manner. "Observe the view."

She went white.

"You – you can see Fergus's patio. . . ."

"On which," he said, "you and he were taking tea."

Kim turned to face him, resigned to hearing some stinging comments but ready also to retaliate. To her amazement she saw on his face an expression of brooding disappointment. It was an expression which vanished at once and she knew she had caught something which he had had no intention of allowing her to see.

Disappointment. The cause? Could it be because she had lied to him? Kim rejected the idea as it was too

145

remote a possibility for acceptance.

"That was detestable," she flashed, deciding it was better to get in the first word. "You deliberately set out to prove me a liar!"

The black brows rose.

"Aren't you a little mixed up? You lied. I had no hand in it."

"You asked questions – Oh, I'm not entering into any arguments! I lied, very well. You'd no right to ask about my movements."

"You're not ashamed of lying?" His eyes never left her face; she once again had the impression that he was disappointed in her. What did it mean? If he was so determined to believe she was a criminal then why should he worry himself about a lie or two? It didn't make sense.

"I lied to save trouble," she confessed,

"So you're afraid of me, eh?"

Her chin lifted.

"I'm not –" She stopped, loath to tell another lie. Her husband's eyes became more penetrating than ever.

"Yes, Kim?" he pressed softly.

She swallowed hard. He took in the pallor of her face, the spasmodic movement of her hands.

"It's – unpleasant, having all these rows," she said defensively. "I hoped to avoid encountering your deplorable temper again."

"My temper? What about yours?"

"You goad me." Her tones were more subdued than she would have liked them to be.

Damon ignored that.

"If you lied to save trouble then surely that is an admittance that you're afraid of me?" She said nothing and after a moment of silence he continued,

146

"You'll be more afraid if you don't keep away from that fellow Smith. Yes, you can flare up if you like, but you should know by now that I'm more than a match for you," he added on noting the light appearing in her eyes, a light which was more than familiar by now. "I have a very good reason for forbidding you to associate with him. Please keep that in mind."

"What reason?" she demanded sharply.

"It needn't concern you." Suddenly, unexpectedly his voice softened a shade. "Just do as I ask. It can't be any hardship for you to keep away from the man." He paused, his gaze probing. "What were you talking about?"

She frowned. Why the interest? And why was he so against her becoming friendly with Fergus, the harmless eccentric who was lonely? Admittedly he himself was not on speaking terms with his neighbour, but Damon had so little interest in his wife that his attitude was exceedingly puzzling.

"All sorts of things. This and that," carelessly and hoping he would be deceived into thinking she was not so afraid of him as he had concluded.

"And what might this and that be?"

Kim was on the point of losing her patience. Afraid of him she was; on the other hand, he did not hold all the aces.

"What we talked about can have no interest for you, Damon. I'm not obliged to report my every move and act to you. I wouldn't be even if we were properly married."

"Properly married?" Amusement now in his voice and expression. She gave a sigh of relief, sure she had escaped further questioning about her visit to Fergus. "Aren't we properly married?"

She was watching his face, puzzled by his expression

147

that had so short a time ago been so threatening.

"What happened to Suzanne?" she asked, and to her surprise her husband actually laughed.

"Not difficult to read your connecting train of thought. Suzanne has nothing at all to do with our marriage, Kim," he told her, and a serious quality had entered his voice all at once. "As you know, we were engaged, but we quarrelled. It is finished."

"Finished?" she breathed, hope surging to engulf all other feeling. "You're not intending to marry her, then?"

"That question's too absurd for answering. I did say, if you remember, that I don't favour divorce." A thin twist of his mouth which was akin to a sneer. "We're a good way behind the times in Greece."

She let this pass. Her heart leapt at the relief his previous words had brought her. Was he telling her, in his own subtle way, that they were to remain married for always? She was fully aware of her subconscious clamouring to remind her that life with Damon would be far from pleasant. There would be too many interludes of fury on his part and fear on hers; added to this he would ever display his mastery – hadn't he already reminded her that the husband was always the master in Greece? His power over her would constantly be exerted; she would never be free from the awareness of his dictatorial qualities.

But her subconscious was swamped and its warnings ignored. Kim found hope a much more pleasant sensation, but of course she refrained from exhibiting any sign of this hope simply because, as yet, there was no indication that Damon would accept her story, much less begin to care a little for her. If only he could care. . . . Her eyes took on a dreamy expression and unconsciously her lips parted, temptingly. If ever he did care, she thought, unable to quell the happiness that surged merely from anticipation, then perhaps there would never be any of those interludes of savagery which she feared, but only happy times when she saw that other man, that sensitive, gentle person who had rescued the flower he had tossed away into the water, and almost tenderly dabbed it dry with his handkerchief.

CHAPTER NINE

THE thing that continued to puzzle Kim was what had happened to Suzanne. The girl had arrived, complete with suitcase, blithely expecting her quarrel with Damon to be made up. What a shock she must have received when he introduced his wife!

So nagging did her curiosity become that in the end Kim asked her husband outright what had happened to his ex-fiancée. The question afforded him some amusement, judging by the sudden twitching of his lips.

"You asked me that before," he reminded her, and she made a little impatient gesture with her hands. She and Damon were in the garden; she had been on her own, strolling about, delighting in the flowers, when to her surprise her husband had come out and joined her.

"You evaded an answer."

"Your curiosity can't be controlled any longer eh?" He stretched forth a hand and plucked a rose, a crimson bud just beginning to open. He looked at it and Kim felt that he was for the moment no longer aware of her presence. He put the flower to his nose absently and moved it to and fro. She watched him, fascinated. What kind of man was he? An enigma, certainly, with many puzzling facets to his nature. "Suzanne's gone home again," he said at last, putting the rose to his nostrils again. "Satisfied?"

"It's only natural that I was curious," she returned defensively. She looked oddly at him, wondering if he were experiencing any emotion at the mention of the girl to whom he had once been engaged. His face was an unreadable mask; his whole attention appeared to be on the lovely creation he held in his hand. Something rather wonderful and exciting stirred within Kim. She saw in her husband a characteristic which she found so endearing that she wished she could lift her face and kiss him. Her thoughts naturally brought a tinge of colour to her cheeks and before she had time to turn away, so that Damon would not notice, a half-smile of quizzical inquiry had replaced the expression-less mask of his face.

"Why the blush?" he asked, twirling the rose by its stem. And, imperatively as she deliberately avoided his eyes by allowing her own to circle the garden, "Look at me!"

With difficulty she met his gaze, afraid lest he should read what she must keep hidden for the time being at least. She lifted a hand to touch her cheek, an unconscious action, as if she would rub away the blush which was causing him to look so searchingly at her.

"I didn't know I was blushing," she said, and saw an instant return of that quizzical smile. How devastatingly attractive he was in this particular mood!

"Another lie, but harmless this time," he said with unexpected gentleness. Kim had the impression that he was being swayed by something quite beyond his control, something which prevented any display of animosity towards her, forcing him instead to treat her as his equal. His next words confirmed this impression.

"Tomorrow, Kim, I'm going into Cos to meet a business associate. Perhaps you'd like to come with me? We shall be lunching aboard the yacht –" He broke off, eyes twinkling. "Or perhaps your memories are too painful?"

Her heart was doing strange things and for a long moment she was unable to speak.

"I'd love to come with you," she murmured at length, her eyes glowing. Damon watched her with an odd expression, then glanced away. Her pulse quickened as with a tug of fear she was caught up in an inner fit of trembling. Was his manner to undergo a change? Would she presently hear him say he had changed his mind about taking her with him into Cos? With swiftly falling spirits she felt instinctively that his offer had been made impulsively, and was already regretted. He did not want her with him, meeting one of his business associates – her, a criminal. That was what he was now thinking, she felt certain of it. Her eyes filled up uncontrollably. The silence became oppressive; it hurt, and she willed him to recapture the smile that only a moment ago had afforded her such pleasure. The silence remained; it demanded breaking, and she spoke the words that reflected her doubts. "You – you do want me to come with you?" There was an undertone of pleading in the question; she had unconsciously begged him not to change his mind.

He turned to her, his hands automatically caressing the soft velvety petals of the rose. She was blinking rapidly and he frowned. Silence reigned once more, a thoughtful silence on his part, but one of breathless waiting for her. So much seemed to depend on his taking her to Cos with him; it would be the first step towards friendship; and following friendship would come affection, and then . . . love? She scarcely dared think of his learning to love her. It was asking too much, she told herself, and yet she was desperate for a change in their relationship.

At length her husband spoke; she grasped at once that he was again swayed by something beyond his control because he allowed his voice to carry an unmistakable note of gentleness and assurance.

"Of course, Kim. I wouldn't have asked you otherwise."

"Thank you," she murmured, and only now, with relief flooding over her, did she become conscious of the nervous perspiration that had dampened the palms of her hands. She had not realized the tension within her had been quite so strong as that.

There was an almost imperceptible return of his smile, before it faded again, but Kim saw it and was satisfied that he was not after all regretting his offer.

"You can wander about, doing some shopping, or anything else you wish, while we talk. Then I suggest you come to the harbour about twelve o'clock and I'll bring you aboard. After lunch I myself have some small items to buy, so we shall be in town for the greater part of the day."

She wandered about the capital after Damon had left her, leaving his car near the harbour and going off to meet his visitor who was arriving on the boat from Piraeus. The lovely public gardens drew her and she revelled in the grand spectacle of exotic flowers and shrubs for a while before strolling along a wide avenue lined on both sides by flowering trees. Pretty villas and bungalows surrounded by their well-kept gardens added to the beauty of the scene. Bananas, pomegranates and lemons grew enticingly close as Kim passed an open space after leaving the houses. Hibiscus formed a hedge along one side of this space, while growing wild were thousands of marigolds and geraniums. A woman passed, carrying a tall package on her head, balancing it with an ease and grace that made Kim gasp. How did the woman manage to stroll along like that without the package toppling down? Smiles were exchanged. Kim said a bright "good morning" and received an equally bright "*kalimera*" in response.

Kim continued to wander, enjoying the sunshine and the flowers and above all the anticipation of meeting Damon at noon.

The Castle of the Knights beckoned enticingly and she went towards it. Its ancient mellowed walls gleamed golden in the sun's flattering rays; bougainvillaea tumbled over its walls. After enjoying the quiet sensation of being in the distant past she crossed the bridge to the square where, by the Turkish mosque, stood the plane tree under which Hippocrates used to instruct his students. It was a gigantic specimen, its gnarled branches twisted in agony-like formations and in many cases supported by stanchions.

At last it was time to make for the harbour and at twelve o'clock prompt Damon was there, on the deck of his yacht. She stepped on board and he introduced her to the short, grey-haired Greek who was just rising from his comfortable chair. What a pleasant place in which to conduct business, thought Kim, extending a hand and murmuring a "How do you do," in response to the man's greeting.

"Your wife is charming, Damon." George Mamoucas looked her over appreciatively. "I'm delighted to be meeting her."

"Thank you." Both Kim and her husband spoke together. She glanced up at him to note the effect of George's remark, but whatever Damon's feelings were he kept them hidden beneath an inscrutable mask.

Damon and his guest had been having a drink on deck, under the shade of a gay striped awning, and as they hadn't finished Kim joined them. She was in a white cotton dress, very simple but smart for all that. Her arms and legs were bare, their rich golden tan making a most attractive contrast to the dress. White sandals and a matching handbag completed a charming picture of beauty and good taste. Without being immodest Kim knew she looked nice, and she did wonder if Damon were deciding that she looked anything but a criminal. Yet what exactly did criminals look like? Elegant gentlemen were often criminals, and beautiful women too.

"Another drink, Kim?" Damon's voice; he was smiling now, and instinctively she knew that he was experiencing a dart of recollection and naturally this brought the colour flooding to her cheeks. Was it on this particular part of the deck that he had thrown that bucket of water over her? She could not help visualizing it and so hot did she become that she could only nod in answer to his question. And then he astounded her by a small gesture that sent her heart racing. He merely patted her hand as it lay on the table. It was nothing, and yet it meant so much. He understood and he was sorry that she had been forced to remember so humiliating a piece of knowledge. She thrilled to his action, telling herself that it must have meaning in that he was now accepting that she was not nearly so bad as he had at first assumed. Perhaps, she thought with ever-increasing optimism, he would very soon now be in a mood to have her repeat her story, and give it much more thought than on its first being related to him when, quite naturally, he had not been in the right frame of mind for its acceptance.

George was a quiet unassuming man, but interesting to talk to. Damon excused himself and went off to speak to one of the hands who was in the galley preparing the lunch and Kim found herself alone with George for a few minutes. He asked how she liked living on the island and very soon the conversation drifted to the interesting topic of the island in general.

The town of Cos itself had been devastated several times by earthquakes, George told her, and each time it had been rebuilt on the ruins which were left.

"That's why the antiquities are so scattered," he explained, "and of course why they are so badly damaged. There were several earthquakes going a long way back in the pre-Christian era," he went on after making sure she was still interested. "Then in 192 A.D. the city was again devastated. This time a magnificent building programme was set in motion and many beautiful buildings arose. There were temples and an amphitheatre, and the thermal baths. You'll probably have been shown the Odeum and Agora and such places by your husband?" She merely nodded and said,

"I've seen those places, yes."

"Well, all this was destroyed in another earthquake about three hundred and fifty years later, but once again it was rebuilt. With the advent of yet another earthquake everything went, owing to the rising of the waters following the actual disaster. The city was abandoned until in the Middle Ages the Knights arrived and built the castle and the walls and gradually another city arose."

"It's a wonder the people would keep on rebuilding. You'd think they would give up hope altogether."

"Eight hundred years had elapsed, remember. No one would bother about an earthquake that had happened so long ago."

"But there was yet another earthquake – after the Italians had occupied the island."

George nodded.

"That's true; it was a mere forty years ago and all that the Italians had done was practically destroyed – and they'd done wonders, I can tell you. However, undaunted, they began to rebuild, but outside the city this time so as to be able to carry out excavations of the ancient ruins unhindered by new buildings, which had hitherto restricted the archaeologists. Also, the new city was rebuilt to resist future earthquakes –"

"This can be done?" she asked unbelievingly, and her companion nodded his head.

"Indeed, yes. There will be no future catastrophes here."

"And so," mused Kim after a while, "that's why we have such wonders to see – because the modern city was built away from the ancient one."

"That's correct –" George broke off as Damon appeared. "We've been having a most interesting discussion," he said with a smile.

"You have?" Dark eyes flickered to Kim, then moved back to George. "About what?"

"The island. Kim is well on the way to becoming a loyal Coan."

"Are you, my dear?" It was a casual question, having no point, and Kim merely gave a small nod of her head. "Lunch is ready," said Damon then, and they all went into the saloon from which, on that other occasion, Damon had curtly ordered her to leave.

She looked at him automatically, then averted her head; he was frowning slightly when presently she sent him another glance. George was saying something amusing; Kim's laughter was instantaneous and the situation was eased. Damon, she felt, had – perhaps for the first time in his life – known a slight tinge of embarrassment at the memory of his treatment of her.

When the meal was over Damon and Kim accompanied George to the landing stage and saw him off. Then they strolled round the shops for a while and by four o'clock they were sitting at a *cafenion* in Liberty Square having afternoon tea, after which they drove home to the villa, having called at Damon's mother's house on the way. She was rapidly improving and so taken with Kim was she that it seemed impossible that Damon would ever upset her by allowing Kim to leave him. Her hopes ran higher than ever.

On arrival at their own home Kim found a letter awaiting her. It was from her foster-mother asking when it would be convenient for her to visit Kim and her husband. On telling Damon of its contents Kim received a glance she failed to analyse. His voice also held an unfathomable note when he said,

"Apart from a couple of days in Athens next week and the week after I shall be at home indefinitely, as far as I know."

She was recalling his advising her not to have her foster-mother stay for long, as a couple of days was sufficient for him to adopt the role of loving husband.

"I'll tell her to come in about a fortnight or three weeks, then?"

He nodded, his cool eyes still expressionless.

"She's coming with her husband, you say?"

"That's right. He's a Greek – I mentioned that, if you remember?"

"What's his name?"

"Pavlos."

"How did she come to marry a Greek?"

"She met him in England, at a friend's house." Kim's reply came with noticeable eagerness, for she

157

was happy at the interest which he was now showing.

"She had been a widow for a good many years and we were delighted at the idea of her getting married at last. She's very happy with Pavlos."

"And she likes living in Athens?"

"Who wouldn't like living in Athens?" The eager exclamation came out involuntarily and it brought a faint smile to her husband's lips.

"I think," he said after a thoughtful pause, "that you had better tell me that story again –"

"Again?" with breathless haste and the appearance of a glowing light in her eyes. "You're willing to listen?"

"Naturally, otherwise why should I request a repetition?"

Kim actually found herself trembling. This was too good to be true!

"And you will believe me?"

At that his expression changed. He replied guardedly,

"It all depends on whether or not I'm convinced, doesn't it?"

A trifle deflated she said,

"It was the truth I told you, Damon."

"I don't remember all of it – not half of it, probably. I was far from being in a receptive mood at that time."

"It was understandable," she admitted. "You had reason to be very angry with me."

"Angry?" with a raising of his brows. "That's mild. You're lucky to be alive."

"I don't believe you'd have turned me over, when I was unconscious in that pond, and left me to drown."

"No?" He was obviously amused as for a long moment he looked down into her face. "How little you

158

know me, my dear. At that particular moment I could have strangled you, let alone merely left you to drown." The swift-as-lightning change in his expression was so startling that Kim felt her breath catch. Her heartbeats began to race – which was ridiculous, she told herself, because she was quite safe now ... or was she? Damon's gaze portrayed sheer uncontrolled savagery and she knew without the smallest doubt that he was reliving those moments when, with what he believed to be a gun prodding into his back, he had been forced to walk in front of her along that lane. What had occurred prior to that had been bad enough for anyone like Damon to endure, but later, when she had viciously butted him to drive him along more quickly ... it must have awakened in him a fury so intense that murder in its most savage form was uppermost in his mind.

"Shall I tell you the story now?" she quivered in sudden haste. "It won't take long."

But it took longer than she expected, because every now and then she would make a long pause, staring into her husband's face, endeavouring to penetrate the in-scrutable mask in an attempt to discover whether or not her story was being received with more credibility than before. But he maintained an uncommunicative expres-sion and each time she found herself floundering a little as she began to join her narrative smoothly. But the breaks weakened the story, she felt sure, and by the time she had finished she was acutely aware of a de-pression of spirits.

"You don't believe me, do you?" she said at last in a hopeless little voice.

He appeared to be lost in intense concentration and, unable to bear the silence any longer Kim interrupted it to tell him that the story would be fully supported by her foster-mother.

"Your foster-mother?" Damon was slowly shaking his head, but Kim gained the impression that the action did not mean what it suggested. She felt that he had not yet decided whether to believe her story or not.

"She could be in league with you," he pointed out.

"She could, yes. But when you've seen her you'll know she isn't."

"My best course then seems to be to reserve judgement until I've seen your foster-mother." He could not fail to notice her disappointment and to her surprise his face softened slightly. "If your story is true," he said almost inaudibly, "then quite a different light is put upon the situation."

She stared at him, in a daze of rapt silence. Her green eyes were alight, but with happiness. She found herself saying in a husky voice,

"You mean – that our marriage might – might be permanent?"

Once again he became guarded. But he was interested in her expression and in the way her words had been spoken. She stared frankly into his piercing dark eyes and saw him swallow hard and there was a strange little movement in the side of his jaw.

"You would like it to be permanent?" he queried at length.

Kim hesitated a moment, half afraid to let him know how she felt. Eventually she said, still looking frankly at him,

"I would ... yes. . . ." and she glanced down then, unable to prolong her gaze. A finger under her chin forced her head up, however, and a profound silence followed while her husband commandingly made her look into his eyes.

"You would," he murmured, and releasing her, he

moved to the other side of the room.

Long silent moments passed; she realized that he wasn't intending to speak any more and she excused herself and left him standing there, looking out of the window to the lovely gardens and the mountain beyond. She had to pass close to him, but he never moved or turned his head. She wondered whether he had noticed her leave the room.

Much later, when she was emerging from the shower-room, she saw him standing in a similar position, but now it was her bedroom window through which he stared and instead of the immaculate clothes he had worn for the meeting with his business associate he now wore a dark blue dressing-gown.

And this time he turned as she moved and a smile softened his mouth; his eyes too wore a softened expression and Kim vividly saw the man with the rose between his teeth – the man who reminded her of a child. But there was nothing childlike about his strength when a moment later he had taken her into his arms. She was crushed to him as passion became unleashed. Yet there was a strange unfamiliar tenderness underlying his ardour, a tenderness she had never before experienced. She responded gladly to his kisses and when he lifted her off her feet she gave a happy contented sigh and buried her face in his shoulder.

CHAPTER TEN

DESPITE the fact that he was still guarded, it was obvious to Kim that her husband was now open-minded as regards her character. It was also clear to her, as the days passed, that he cared for her, but to what extent she found it impossible to assess. Sometimes she caught glimpses of what she happily decided was real love, but just as she was allowing her hopes to soar he would change unaccountably and she would be left wondering what she had done to bring about his cool indifference towards her. At these times she would dejectedly tell herself that it was still as a pillow friend that he regarded her and, spurred by disappointment and humiliation, she would retaliate by herself adopting a distant manner.

She had gone off in a temper one day and, on meeting Fergus in the lane, had defiantly accepted his invitation to have tea with him. As before they took it on the patio and as before they were seen by Damon. On her return Kim had come in for the full brunt of his fury, and his threats had left her trembling but still defiant. What sort of a life would they lead were they both to decide to remain together? It would soon become unbearable, she admitted in a spate of despair. Far better to cut the tie as soon as possible than drag on until real hatred set in.

Damon's attitude towards Fergus was to her mind absolutely ridiculous, and somehow it detracted from the fineness of his character as she knew it. To object to so harmless a man seemed both uncharitable and petty. The man was an eccentric, it was true; he had offended his neighbour by building a monstrosity which would naturally upset anyone with an ounce of love for the landscape and the view. Fergus had obligingly taken down his tower, so why should Damon not treat him as he should be treated – as a rather odd, but harmless acquaintance?

She had pointed this out, but had received only an imperious,

"Keep away! If you continue to defy me you're

going to feel sorry for yourself. I've warned you, Kim, and if you've any sense you'll heed that warning."

This was of course as a red rag to a bull and had Fergus been at home she would instantly have gone along to visit him. But he was away; she had seen his car at the harbour, and as it had been there for two days she knew he was away from home. She thought he must be in Athens and wondered if he had friends there. He had given her the impression of having no real friends and the fact that he was away from home surprised her.

On the Tuesday before her foster-mother was expected the following weekend Damon announced his attention of going to the capital. He would be away until Thursday, he said, and for a moment Kim almost asked if she could go with him. However, she refrained, admitting that their relationship, though more pleasant for the most part than in the past, had not reached that stage of intimacy when she could expect her husband to trouble himself that she might be lonely, at home on her own.

He had just left when she saw Fergus's car roll along his drive. He got out and as she watched she saw him stand and look around, almost furtively. She smiled in some amusement. Did he think someone was watching him?

He ambled into the house, via the patio, and Kim turned away from the window. To her surprise he came along about half an hour later as she sat on the lawn with a book. He stood at the other side of the hedge and called to her.

"Hello there. How about coming over to my place for elevenses?"

"You know my husband's away?" she asked curiously, and he nodded.

"I – er – saw him at the airport."

"Oh, I see."

"I'd appreciate your company."

"All right." She rose and went round to the gate, leaving her book on the chair. "You've been away yourself?"

"I went to England. A distant relation had died and I had to attend the funeral. That's why I'm glum – have you noticed? I detest funerals almost as much as I detest weddings. Both are so infinitely depressing because they both spell doom – There I go! Are you still in love with that arrogant man?"

"Damon? Of course." How was it, she wondered, that she could never be cross with Fergus? If anyone else said a word of disparagement about her husband she would jump on them. But Fergus was so very nice – just a big baby really, mischievous but with no real harm in him.

He came round to the gate and opened it for her to pass through. They strolled together along the lane and entered his drive. A couple of bright blue and red gnomes grinned at them from yellow toadstools set beneath a tree made of iron. Its branches were all holed right the way along their length and when a tap was turned on the branches dripped with artificial rain. Pride had brought a glow to Fergus's face when he demonstrated for her one day, and the wings at the sides of his eyebrows had fluttered so that Kim just had to burst out laughing.

"Sit on the patio," he invited when they were in his garden proper. "I'll get the coffee." He went off and she sat comfortably in the shade of the vines, gazing at the extraordinary miscellany of objects with which Fergus had surrounded himself. It was in a way no wonder that Damon was so critical. Nevertheless, he should be more understanding, Kim decided, and hoped that quite soon she could break down the barrier between the two near neighbours. For during the past few days – ever since Damon had made her retell her story, in fact – he had been different with her. True, some days had been far from perfect, since he would withdraw from her and she would find herself alone for a few hours, but other days had been idyllic for her, as she seemed without effort to get close to her husband, and her optimism for a happy future would rise to dizzy heights. "There –!" Fergus put the tray on the table and sat down. His big blue eyes smiled benignly as he began to pour the coffee. "How long will your husband be away?" he inquired casually after a while.

"Until Thursday." She stopped and listened. "The phone," she said, but Fergus was already rising to his feet.

He was away a long time and she got up and wandered about among the follies. A path made of cobblestones painted in different colours led to somewhere she had not seen before and she strolled along it. It wound about and at one point came close to one of the windows of the villa. Although the window was closed she heard Fergus's voice, and she gave a gasp of disbelief.

He was actually shouting at whoever it was on the other end of the line!

The gentle harmless Fergus . . . shouting in anger.

The voice stopped and Kim sped back to her chair on the patio, looking up and eyeing Fergus curiously as he came from the house a moment later, stepping through the french window on to the patio. His benign cheeks were flushed, his big blue eyes glinting strangely. But on noting her interest he smiled and sat down and inquired anxiously if her coffee were cold.

"You should have drunk it," he added, picking up the pot. "There was no need to wait for me."

"It isn't cold," she assured him, her eyes still on his face. "You look worried," she added. "Is something wrong?"

He gave her a smile of disarming mildness and shook his head.

"No, my dear, there's nothing at all wrong. My grocer's just been on the phone to tell me I owe him five hundred *drachmae*, but I assured him it was now in the post. More coffee, Kim?"

"Yes, please." His grocer ... Fergus really was shouting, loudly and angrily. Kim had naturally not listened to any actual words, but she had the impression that someone was receiving a good telling off.

Fergus leant forward to pour her coffee, but one hand lay resting on the table and as she watched Kim saw it close, fist-tight, so that the knucklebones shone palely beneath the tanned skin. Damon's fist sometimes closed like that, when he was suppressing an inner fury.

"So your husband is away until Thursday? You'll be lonely on your own. Come over and have dinner with me this evening. I can cook a little, when I have a guest, so don't think you'll be given sandwiches." He grinned and the wings sprouted on his eyebrows. "Do you like music?"

"Of course."

"Then after dinner we can listen to records. You'll come?"

She hesitated, unable to fathom out a reason for her uncertainty.

"I'll think about it, Fergus, and ring you this afternoon," she decided at last.

"You can't make up your mind now?" He looked a trifle upset and went on to remind her that she had once almost promised to attend a barn dance, should he decide to have one. "Coming to dinner isn't much different," he pointed out, and as she still found no reason for her hesitancy she smiled and promised to come to dinner.

But there was an uneasiness about her as she dressed; she kept on hearing that angry voice, which was so far removed from anything she would ever have expected from the mild and inoffensive Folly Man, as he had termed himself. Somehow, Kim felt there was something wrong with the whole set-up – and yet what could be wrong? The man was as transparent as anyone possibly could be – "But I'm sure he lied about that call. I'm sure it wasn't his grocer to whom he was speaking."

However, Kim kept her promise and actually enjoyed the meal Fergus had prepared. He spoke of new projects – an orangery with masses of wrought iron embellishments was his latest idea, and as he had intimated that he was not over-endowed with money she did venture to ask if he could afford it.

"These Greeks work for small sums. Yes, I shall just be able to manage it – I think."

She laughed and asked where it was to be.

"I hope it won't be too conspicuous," she said.

"I'll have it on the other side of the shrubbery. You won't see it from your house." All the time he talked Kim had the impression that his mind was elsewhere, although there was nothing at all in his manner to indicate this.

After dinner they listened to his records for a while and then Kim said she must be leaving.

"I'll walk with you," he offered. "It's too dark for

167

you to go home alone."

Kim made no objection and together they walked slowly along the lane. On reaching the front door of the villa Kim turned to say goodnight.

"And thank you for a most appetising meal, Fergus," she smiled. "As you said, you can cook."

He seemed almost childishly pleased and, to her astonishment and embarrassment, he raised her hand to his lips and kissed it gently.

"You're a very kind young woman, Kim. Thank you for your company this evening. Perhaps I shall see you tomorrow. Will you be taking a walk?"

"Some time during the day, yes. I'll call if I see you about anywhere."

"Thanks." He looked at the darkened windows of the villa. "You're not all alone, I hope?"

"Elene will be back later; she's gone to see her mother."

"Damon Souris has a man as well? I'm sure I've seen one around."

"That's right, but Andreas doesn't live in."

"I see." Fergus seemed reluctant to leave. Kim's heart went out to him suddenly. He was lonely and in consequence he was prolonging the time spent in her company. "It's early," he said hesitantly, looking at her with what could only be described as a plea. "If Elene's not expected back yet you could ask me in for a drink —" He shook his head and stepped back, down one of the steps. "No, I'm sorry, Kim; I shouldn't have asked that of you."

"There'd be no harm in your having a drink, Fergus." She fitted her key into the door. "Come on in. Elene will be an hour or more yet."

"Pity your husband's fallen out with me," he said after thanking her and following her into the house. "I

168

think that, on his return, I'll come over and see if I can put things right between us."

"I wish you would, Fergus, because then you would be able to visit us, and it wouldn't be so lonely for you."

He nodded, taking the chair she indicated.

"You're right. Yes," he decided, "I'll come over on Thursday evening – if he's in early enough – and apologize."

After dropping her key in her handbag Kim put the bag on a chair and asked Fergus what he would have.

"Brandy, dear, and water, if you please."

"You pour what you want while I get the water."

On her return from the kitchen Kim was surprised to see that he was just picking up the brandy.

"I've been looking round," he admitted on noting her curious expression. "Your husband's a collector."

"The antiques? Yes, he does collect."

Fergus grinned at her as she poured the water into the glass he was holding out.

"Not of follies, either. Those Chelsea groups are delightful – and I envy him his early Worcester. That's of the Dr. Wall period – very rare mark, it has."

"You've picked it up?" Somehow she was relieved to find that he was speaking the truth when he said he had been looking around. Yet what else could he have been doing while she was away in the kitchen? There was nothing – and yet she had been uneasy on noting that he had not been doing what she expected him to do, which was to pour out his brandy.

"Yes, I hope you don't mind?"

"I don't know. . . . If it were to get broken. . . ?"

"You'd be in trouble with your husband! My dear I'm used to handling such treasures. I did have that member of the aristocracy for my relative, as you know, I often visited his home."

"I'm sorry. I should have known you know how to handle these things, for otherwise you wouldn't have touched them."

Half an hour later he was leaving. And as she closed the door behind him Kim found herself breathing a sigh of relief. That poor lonely man. Why should she be so relieved to see him go?

It was a week later; Damon came from his study, where he had been speaking on the telephone, which had rung a few moments earlier, and on seeing his expression Kim felt her breath catch.

"Your mother," she faltered, "she's had a relapse?"

"No – thank God it isn't that!" He looked at Kim, but was a long way off. "One of our offices has been robbed," he said at last. "Not mine, but one of the firm's."

"The firm's?" Kim had never been told the source of her husband's income.

"My company own a chain of hotels – among other things – and once a year we pay a large bonus to our employees. This is made up at one central office and distributed to the hotel managers to give out to their staffs. Just for one day and night in the year is this large sum of money lying in that office. Whoever broke in last night knew of this." Damon's face was grey and drawn. Kim was puzzled at the obvious intensity of his feelings as she naturally assumed that the insurance company would stand the loss. She mentioned this to him and he nodded instantly.

"Then why are you so dreadfully worried? I know it *is* worrying," she hastily added, "but there's no actual loss to your firm?"

He looked at her, a nerve in his neck pulsating madly.

"Apart from the man in charge of that office," he said slowly, "I am the only one in possession of a key. And whoever entered last night entered with a key."

Kim stared; the full content of his words not immediately taking on the significance he had meant to convey.

"That's impossible. No, he must have picked the lock."

"He entered with a key."

Bewilderedly she looked at him.

"They can't suspect you. Why, I can vouch for your being here all last night."

"My dear girl, you're my wife."

"They wouldn't believe me?"

"No, they wouldn't believe you."

She spread her hands, still mystified.

"What good would it do you to rob yourself?"

"I'd be robbing the firm – and the insurance company will pay, as you've just remarked."

"They can't suspect you!" she exclaimed indignantly. "It's impossible! The man must have got a key from somewhere, that's obvious!"

"To me – and, it seems to you, my dear. But will it be obvious to the police?"

She went white.

"They wouldn't t-take you away," she faltered, her heart thudding uncomfortably. "They wouldn't dare – not you!"

Faintly he smiled.

"The police will most certainly suspect me. Whether or not they'll arrest me remains to be seen. There is another man with a key, so at the moment two of us are suspect."

"It must be the other man," she declared firmly. "There's no doubt about it!"

"This man has been with the firm for over thirty years and has a blameless record. I have been with this firm for only a year. It was bought up by my company, but the employees all remained. No, Kim, it is not this other man. I myself would swear to it."

"Then the robber got the key from him at some time or another and had one taken off it."

Damon said nothing. He was deep in thought, his face still grey and drawn. Kim's eyes filled; she was more afraid than she had ever been in her life, even when her husband had been in his most savage mood. Damon taken away from her. . . .

"What can we do?" she said urgently, feeling something *could* be done, if only they could decide on some sort of action.

But Damon was shaking his head.

"There's nothing we can do but wait for the visit from the police."

What small vestige of colour remained instantly left her cheeks.

"The police are coming here?"

"They're flying over in a special plane. They should be arriving within the next hour or so."

Never had a wait seemed so long. Kim was at last unable to stand it any longer and she sprang up from her chair and said,

"Can we go for a walk or something? I can't bear it, Damon —" and she started to cry, putting her face in her hands. "They c-can't p-possibly pin such a crime on – on you."

He came to her and his arm went round her shoulders.

"Tears," he murmured almost to himself. "Tears for me – and not once have you shed tears for yourself, not even when you were in such pain. . . ."

She twisted in his arm and his other arm came round her.

"I love you, Damon," she whispered, quite unable to hold it back in this – what appeared to be – so dire a situation. "I c-can't help loving you."

A small laugh forced itself from his lips.

"There's no need to be apologetic about it, my dear." He paused a moment and looked down into her tear-stained face. Strength in plenty she possessed, Damon had had proof of that over and over again, but as she rested in the circle of his arms now there was a helplessness about her that brought out all the chivalry he possessed and she was caught gently to him and his mouth came down on hers, comfortingly, and when presently he held her from him she was left in no doubt at all that she too was loved. She wanted to speak, to ask him if he now believed her story, which he must, obviously, or otherwise he could not love her. But this was not the time for wanting to hear from his own lips the words she had been longing to hear since the moment when, realizing she was deeply affected by him, she began to ask herself the reason for this strange new feeling that possessed her.

"Can we walk?" she repeated. "I'll feel better if I'm doing something."

"Very well." Elene was out shopping and Andreas had not put in an appearance that day as he had asked for time off to attend to his own garden and lemon orchard. "Have you your key handy? Mine's in my bedroom."

"Yes, it's here in my bag." With trembling fingers she fumbled with the clasp. Her nerves were all to pieces, she realized as she searched for her front door key. "It isn't here. . . ." A frown crossed her brow as she tried to concentrate. When did she last have the key?

It was some time ago, as for the past week she had gone out only with Damon and he had used his own key when necessary, which was not often since Elene was almost always somewhere about. "It isn't here," she repeated blankly.

"Then it's somewhere else, obviously. Never mind, I'll fetch mine." He was gone and she tried once again to concentrate, but her mind was filled with one thing – the fear for her husband. Surely an innocent man could not be charged with a crime. It had happened before, though, and rare though it was, innocent men had actually been convicted.

She closed her bag and laid it on the couch as Damon re-entered the room.

"Ready?" he asked, then added with a frown, "Kim, there's no need for such anxiety at this stage. Now, just stop it, do you hear?"

She nodded dumbly, and he took her hand as they left the house. They had only reached the end of the drive, however, when the police car arrived. Her heart gave a great lurch and for a moment she felt her senses must surely leave her.

"Go back, dear, and stay in your room – or wander about the garden – and stop worrying!" he added sternly as tears filled her eyes.

She stood aside as the car passed, Damon having got into the back seat after a few words spoken in Greek had passed between him and the man seated by the driver. Would he be in the car when it left – taken to Athens for questioning?

For a while she wandered about aimlessly, then went to her bedroom. She sank weakly on to the bed and tears filled her eyes again. A knock on the door brought her to her feet and she hastily dried her eyes.

"The gentlemen would like to speak to you, Mrs.

174

Damon." Elene's voice held a scared note and her gaze was curious as she saw the evidence of Kim's recent tears.

"Me —?" The exclamation was out before she could check it, but she recovered instantly, resuming her dignity as she told Elene she would be along in a few minutes.

What could they want with her? Kim shook her head bewilderedly and proceeded to bathe her face and apply a little colour to her cheeks and mouth.

The three men stood up as she entered the lounge; they were all eyeing her curiously as she moved across the room to take a chair by her husband. The men sat down; it was a tense atmosphere and Kim became part of it — so much a part of it that her nerves tingled and the fine gold hairs on her forearms stood up, away from her flesh. She felt an icy chill pass right through her body.

"We've discovered that someone has been in here, Kim," Damon began, when he was interrupted, firmly but at the same time respectfully, as one of the police officers said,

"We believe someone has entered this house, Mrs. Souris, but it has certainly not been established that this is so." He paused a moment. "The key which your husband has in his possession — the key to the office which has been robbed — is kept in his safe in his study. That key was removed from the safe and a wax impression taken of it."

"A wax impression?" she repeated dazedly. "But that's impossible. No one could get in here." What did it all mean? And why were they telling her this?

"Your husband tells us you have mislaid your front door key. Can you find it, do you think?"

She started, having forgotten all about her key . . .

and that start was not lost on any of the three men sitting there. For no reason at all she blushed, and because they stared so she averted her head.

"I'll go and see if – if it's in one of my other bags," she stammered, and as one of the officers nodded she got to her feet and left the room.

Her key. . . . She hadn't used any of these bags recently, and it was an automatic response when she tipped the contents of each one on to the bed. Her pockets . . . she had only two, in her coat. . . . Not there. Not in any of the drawers. . . . Her concentration was weak and no matter how hard she tried to think she found that waves of fear and bewilderment were infiltrating to blank out clear vision. Terrified of returning to the lounge, she delayed by standing by the window and staring out across the garden to the lane.

Her attention was caught by the ambling figure. Fergus. . . . He was glancing along the drive. Could he see the police car? She hoped he could not – Fergus!

She knew now when last she had used her key, and she frowned as she tried to think what she had done with it after bringing Fergus into the house that evening.

"I'm sure I dropped it into my bag – but I couldn't have, because otherwise it would be there now!" Could she have put it on a table or a chair? And could Fergus – absent-minded as he sometimes was – have picked it up and put it in his pocket? If so then someone must have stolen it from him. . . . At this stage Kim's mind, still too dazed for any real picture to emerge, was occupied only by the matter of her lost key, and without thinking she left the house by the side door and raced along the lane after Fergus. He had entered his garden before she got close enough to be able to call out without the risk of attracting the attention of the three men in the villa.

Fergus turned, and a mild sort of smile touched his lips. The big blue eyes were questioning as he waited for her to come up to where he was standing, by the patio steps.

"Fergus," she gasped, taking a deep gulp of air, "do you remember the night I took you into our lounge for a drink?"

"I couldn't forget it, my dear. You made a lonely man happy that night. I –"

Impatiently she interrupted him, fearful that even now her husband would have gone along to her bedroom to see what was keeping her.

"My door key – I can't find it, Fergus, and it's terribly important that I do find it!" She stopped for breath, even now not conscious of the fact that the finding of the key was not really of vital importance. "I used it that night and haven't used it since. I thought I'd put it away in my handbag, but I didn't. I must have put it down somewhere and I'm wondering if you – unintentionally, of course – happened to pick it up and put it in your pocket?"

"I don't think so." He looked curiously at her. "Is there some urgency?" His eyes flickered to the villa, then back to Kim's flushed face.

"Yes – yes, there is! Please, Fergus, go and look in your pockets!"

"Of course, my dear." But, maddeningly, he did not move. There was something very strange about his manner, she noticed, but vaguely, as her mind was frantically willing him to go and do her bidding. "Do you mind telling me what this urgency is?" She was beginning to shake her head when he added, "I saw a police car outside your house as I passed just now . . .?"

She sagged.

"Fergus, please don't ask me any questions, but just go and see if you have my key!"

"The police want the key?" Fergus still made no move to enter the house.

She actually gritted her teeth. Why was the man so infuriating! Why couldn't he do as he was told?

"Yes," she admitted resignedly, "they do."

He regarded her speculatively from the depth of those baby blue eyes.

"Well, my dear, I'll have a look, but I'm quite sure I never touched your key. Er – have you had a robbery, or something, that you have the police at your house?"

"The key," she groaned. "Go and look, Fergus, *please*!" Damon must surely have gone along to her room by now, she decided, frantically trying to visualize what was going on over there.

"Come in," he invited. "No, not in the lounge – the air's so sultry in there. Don't know why the builder faced it south. In here, where it's cool. Sit down, Kim, while I go and search my pockets."

She drew a deep breath when at last he went from the room, and she let her breath out slowly, in an attempt to crush her impatience. As if it mattered in which room she waited! For the first time she admitted that there was something actually stupid about Fergus. So stupid, she thought, that it could almost be an act – An act. . . . Suddenly her heart gave a sickening jerk that was a prelude to enlightenment, as, flooding in, came so many puzzling incidents. That angry voice which she would never have associated with the mild and inoffensive Folly Man; that flush on his face and those glinting eyes; the clenched fist that had reminded her of Damon's similar action when he was suppressing an inner fury. She recalled her own uneasiness, her puzzlement when on bringing in that water he had

178

asked for she found that he had not poured his brandy. He'd been looking round, he had said. Was that water really necessary, or had he asked for it merely to get her out of the room, while he took the key from her handbag? She recollected that Fergus had asked how long Damon would be away. He would know the coast was clear, as it were, both on Tuesday and Wednesday nights. Kim frowned. Surely either she or Elene would have heard if he had entered the house? But Elene's room was away behind the kitchen, where she also had a small sitting-room. And her own bedroom was a long way from Damon's study – at the opposite side of the house, in fact, and at the furthest possible point from the front door. She shook her head. It didn't seem possible that Fergus could be the robber, the man who had taken a wax impression of the key of the office. Yet it all pointed to him – Her thoughts cut off as the door closed and the key was turned in the lock. She flung herself across the room and tugged at the handle.

"Let me out of here! What's the idea?"

"That damned husband of yours is on his way! How I hate him – smug in his wealth, which comes so damned easy, from the labours of others! I hate him, I tell you!"

"You're mad!" she called, and bedlam resulted. Fergus hammered on the door panels with his fists.

"He's suspected me for a while, I've sensed it. But he'll never send me to jail – never!"

"Where's my wife!" Imperious the voice, from just outside the door. "She came here, I saw her running when I went to her room to see what had happened to her, so you needn't tell me she isn't in this house."

"Yes, she's here – in this room –" Again the panels were thumped. "And you won't have her back un-harmed until we've talked business and concluded it in a way that suits me."

"So you admit breaking into our office?"

No answer. When Fergus spoke eventually it was to say,

"If you go to the police you'll be convicting your wife as well. She's a crook herself; she told me about her life and the way she and her confederates kidnap wealthy men and hold them to ransom –"

"It's a lie!" cried Kim frantically. "Damon, don't believe a word he says!"

"Carry on, Smith." The cold unemotional voice smote Kim's ears and a terrible despair flooded over her. Surely Damon wouldn't believe that she had helped Fergus by giving him the key? Yet such a conclusion was only natural, and as she listened to Fergus relating all she had told him in confidence, believing him to be so harmless, and so friendly, she found every vestige of hope deserting her.

"She assisted me in this job, giving me the key to get into the house when she and Elene were out the following afternoon. She had told me they'd be out –"

"I never did! You must have spied, just as you've always spied on our house and movements. I see that now!"

"She told me the office key was in the safe; I hadn't much difficulty with the safe, by the way, and I advise you to get that new one just out. The office safe was rather more difficult, but as a cracksman I managed it very well. I've dealt successfully with much more complicated locks." He was suave now and all anger appeared to have dissolved. "Now, Souris, do we talk business or not?"

Another silence and then,

"Do you think I would hamper the course of justice?"

"Not because of your wife, no," he said, and Kim's heart contracted with an almost physical pain. "You don't love her, that's obvious, seeing the circumstances of your marriage –"

"My wife confided that in you also?"

"She confided in me wholly. We were planning the robbery, remember –"

"We weren't! Oh, Damon, I beg of you, don't heed him!" If only she had taken more notice of her husband when he forbade her to visit Fergus; if only she hadn't been so defiant. But it was too late now for regrets; by her own stupidity she had ruined her whole life, for no matter what the outcome of this Damon would never be able to forgive her. To have confided so much to this despicable creature – who had, it seemed, always hated Damon, and for no valid reason that Kim could see. Even Mrs. Souris had been deceived, though, so Kim did feel a sudden easing of her mind, but ever such a slight easing.

"You and she planned the robbery?" Damon's voice repeating what Fergus had said, just as if there had been no pleading interruption from his wife. "She gave you the key, you say?"

"Correct. And so you see she is condemned with me if you go back and bring the police here. Are you willing to stand the disgrace – and to jeopardize your mother's life?"

"You appear to know just about everything there is to know," sneered Damon, but the disillusionment in his voice could not possibly escape his wife.

"Naturally. Kim told me it all."

"What is it you want?" at last in a voice of resignation, and a triumphant laugh escaped the man to whom the question was put.

"You can take your wife back with you only if you

181

promise to say absolutely nothing of your suspicions."

"That would be a criminal offence on my part."

"Who'll ever know? I want to keep the cash, by the way. The insurance company will make it good." Kim heard that much, but then she turned at the tapping on the window, and there, incredible though it was, stood her foster-mother!

Kim put a hand to her lips as Mumsie would have spoken. The window was screwed down, so there was no chance of opening it. Had there been Kim would long since have escaped and gone to the villa to fetch the police.

"Darling, how did you get here?" gasped Kim when she had recovered from her astonishment. She spoke very quietly, but to her relief her mother could make out what she was saying.

"I came on ahead of Pavlos – two days ahead of him. What's going on, though? I rang the bell, but no one answered. Is it not in working order? Come and open the door for me –"

"Mumsie darling –" Kim put her mouth to the glass and asked her again how she came to be here.

"I've told you, I came on ahead –" Once again Kim interrupted.

"But why are you *here* – at this house?"

"Because it's your house, of course," blankly, and then, "Kim, is anything wrong? Why don't you come out of there?"

"Our house? You thought this was my husband's house?"

"This is where the taxi-man dropped me. He had another fare along with me – it was cheaper for us both, you see, and this other fare was going to the next village."

"Never mind that," interrupted Kim impatiently.

And she went on to explain as briefly as she could. "It's a miracle that you're here, but don't ask any more questions. Just do as I say and bring those two policemen over to this house."

"Kim, love," said Mumsie, shaking her head, "you do get yourself into some scrapes. I must tell your husband to keep a close watch on you –"

"Darling," exasperatedly and in a voice that should never have been used to utter an endearment, "do as I ask!"

Yes, it was a miracle that Mumsie had gone to the wrong house, Damon was saying in some amusement a couple of hours later as he and Kim sat on the couch in the lounge.

"You've said it at least half a dozen times, darling."

She laughed shakily, still unable to believe that everything was all right between her husband and herself. But he had been so very understanding and forgiving, especially when she explained that it had been because of Suzanne that she had been tempted to confide in Fergus.

"I was so scared that you'd want to marry her, and I talked to Fergus, for comfort."

"You had no need to be scared, my precious. For I already loved you at that time."

"If only I'd known," she said regretfully. "I could think only of a reunion between you, and – and I needed – needed company. There was only Fergus –" Damon had brought her close to his hard body and the rest was smothered by his kiss.

Now, as she sat very close to him on the couch, with the late afternoon sun slanting through the window, Kim looked at him with a dreamy gaze, her face aglow with a light that was a mingling of happiness and gratitude and disbelief.

"It was a million to one chance," she began, when her husband interrupted with,

"Yes, pet, it was a million to one chance – which is just the same as a miracle."

She laughed again, apologetically.

"It's just that I couldn't believe my eyes when I saw her there. Don't you think she's the dearest darling?" she asked, abruptly veering the question as her thoughts flitted about in all directions.

"I most certainly think she is the dearest darling," was her husband's grave response, and Kim immediately accused him of teasing her.

"Were you really going to consider Fergus's ultimatum?" she asked as yet another thought thrust in to eclipse the others temporarily.

"Kim, sweetheart, don't ask me that. I really don't know what I would have done. My sense of honour forbade my accepting his ultimatum, but on the other hand I had both you to think of and my mother. It was Mother mostly, though," he added, "because I knew you were, in the main, innocent. Anything you'd done was done against me personally –"

"My stupid defiance? Yes, and I'm so sorry, Damon. I should have known you had a good reason."

"I'd had my suspicions that all that nonsense was just a pose. Those eyebrows – it was obvious to me that they were false – just part of the whole ridiculous make-up."

"I wanted to laugh when the policeman grabbed him and one fell off! But of course it wasn't the right time for humour." She gave a small sigh. "I always thought I was so clever, but I was an idiot where Fergus was concerned. I felt so sorry for him I would have found him a wife if I could."

Damon merely smiled at this, and said after a pause,

"I myself considered him to be harmless at first, but he flaunted his eccentricities so much that I became suspicious. Of course, I had no idea he was a wanted man and that his eccentricities were all part of the disguise. He was clever, I'll give him that. For by drawing attention to himself he naturally allayed any suspicions, since criminals usually lie low."

"But you were suspicious of him."

"I had doubts about his integrity. Also, our local policeman was vaguely suspicious of him because he found out, quite by accident, that Smith wasn't his real name. A friend — or," amended Damon with a teasing smile, "an accomplice greeted him on arrival at the airport and the name this fellow used was Burgess."

"And our local policeman told you?"

"He was looking for glory; he asked me to keep an eye on Smith and report. Of course, I had more important things to do."

Kim recalled Fergus's anger when speaking on the telephone and wondered if he were rating one of his confederates who had made a mistake. She would never know, and it didn't matter anyway. It was all over and done with, and although there would be other minor details that would crop up from time to time she and Damon had for the most part cleared up all the mysteries and misunderstandings of the past few weeks.

Thoughts flitted about again and she asked, looking rather coyly at him from under her lashes,

"On the yacht, Damon — did you know what to do with me?"

"What to do with you?"

"I mean — the punishment? I had the impression that you wished you'd never bothered to bring me aboard, because, having done so, you didn't know what you were going to do with me."

He laughed and admitted that he did in fact regret having succumbed to the angry impulse and brought her on to his yacht.

"But I have no regrets now," he murmured close to her cheek, and she turned right round then and slipped into his inviting arms and her head came to rest against his shoulder.

"Damon."

"My dearest?"

"You were saying, when I interrupted you, that you knew I was innocent. How could you, when Fergus was giving you all that damning evidence?"

"He said that you gave him the key."

She looked up from her most comfortable position and showed him a blank expression.

"Well?"

"Had you been in league with him then there was no necessity for you to hand him over the key. You would naturally have let him into the house yourself, without putting him to the trouble, and the risk, of illegal entry. That was the slip which proved your innocence, my love."

To his surprise she shuddered against him.

"It was a miracle," she breathed, "a million to one chance." And she stopped then and joined in his laughter. "Sorry, darling, I'm not being very original today, am I?"

He agreed readily, but added with some humour both in his eyes and in his voice,

"You *are* under a rather strong emotional strain, though, so it's understandable."

She snuggled close again and asked the question that she had wanted to ask for some time.

"Were you ever really in love with Suzanne?"

"I don't think so," casually after a slight hesitation. "Suzanne certainly wasn't in love with me. She admitted right at the start that she wanted to marry for money. I rather liked her honesty — and she was pretty too. Also, Mother had been on for some time about my getting married and settling down to the raising of a family, and as I was beginning myself to think it was time I married Suzanne seemed a suitable choice."

So much for that. Kim's cup of happiness was full to the brim. She had been just a little perturbed about his feelings for Suzanne, and yet, come to think of it, she herself had earlier concluded that there was no love of any depth between them, for had there been they must surely have been eager to get married.

Damon was kissing his wife passionately when the door opened and Mumsie stood on the threshold.

"Oh, shall I come back later?" she inquired with what was plainly well-feigned artlessness.

"If it's not important," laughed Damon, lifting his dark head, "yes."

"Damon! Mumsie's our honoured guest!"

Mumsie came into the room and stood looking down at them. They had told her some of the story but not all — just enough to satisfy her curiosity and to convince her that her beloved Kim was happy in her marriage.

"It is rather important, Damon." She had been in the room given her by Kim and she was looking more than a little pretty after her shower and the trouble she had obviously taken in her choice of clothes.

"It is? Well, sit down and let us hear it."

"It's Kim. You'll appreciate that she's clever at getting herself into scrapes?"

"Mrs. Marcoras," said Damon, lips quivering, "you

have made the understatement of the year. She isn't merely clever, she's a genius! "

"Well then, I've been thinking. Will you promise me you'll keep an eye on her? I shall feel much easier in my mind if I have your promise."

"I shall never allow her out of my sight," he returned gravely, and Mumsie's eyes lit with laughter.

"You're a tease, I can see. Nevertheless, you will have to watch her. She has always had what we all called 'unorthodox notions', and I should hate her to find herself in trouble again."

"Mumsie darling," interposed Kim with a laugh, "I've finished with adventures for ever. Does that satisfy you?"

Her foster-mother smiled happily.

"Yes, dear, it does. And now, if you'll excuse me, I'm going back to my room to finish my unpacking."

Damon gazed tenderly into his wife's eyes as the door softly closed.

"You haven't finished with adventure," he said, taking her face in his hands and kissing her eager lips over and over again. "You're just starting on an adventure that's going to last for the rest of your life."

"The adventure of love," she murmured, and felt her husband's heart begin to throb madly against her own.

Golden Harlequin $1.95 per vol.
Each Volume Contains 3 Complete Harlequin Romances

☐ Volume 10

FOUR ROADS TO WINDRUSH by Susan Barrie   (No. 687)
Lindsay wasn't sure she could endure this much longer, after all, this "house" where she was now employed, was once her own home. Old Mr. Martingale had been a delight to work for, then the new owner came — a tyrant, a martinet — a brute.

SURGEON FOR TONIGHT by Elizabeth Houghton   (No. 724)
Jan was about to enter a marriage which would salve her conscience, but break her heart. Dr. Ritchie, a man who found little time for play, and even less for women, had the power to spare her this heartbreak, if only he could become "human" enough, and in time . . . .

THE WILD LAND by Isobel Chace   (No. 821)
The little town of Les Saintes de la Mer. The annual gathering of gypsies from all over Europe. When Emma was summoned to France to visit her grandmother, she was not prepared for all this excitement, and even less prepared for Charles Rideau!

☐ Volume 11

NURSE OF ALL WORK by Jane Arbor   (No. 690)
When everyone around her seemed to shun her, there was Glen Fraser, the new Welfare Officer. Nurse Nightingale was grateful to him, it would indeed have been so easy to love him, but for the unsuperable barrier which stood between them . . . .

HOUSE OF THE SHINING TIDE by Essie Summers   (No. 724)
Lorette — a perfect nuisance to her stepsister, was finally going to be off Judith's hands, so, to keep Lorette's engagement together, Judith did everything possible. Ironically, it was through the troublesome Lorette that Judith herself found the key to a lasting happiness.

ALL I ASK by Anne Weale   (No. 830)
To heal a broken heart, Francesca decided she must "get away". Wisely, she chose the remote Andorra, in the heart of the Pyrenees. Was it equally as wise however, for her to remain in the orbit of the attractive Nicholas de Vega.

Golden Harlequin $1.95 per vol.
Each Volume Contains 3 Complete Harlequin Romances

☐ # Volume 16

LOVE HIM OR LEAVE HIM by Mary Burchell (No. 616)
In anger — he fired her, later to find that he desperately needed her help. Anne volunteered, and what began as a generous gesture, developed into a situation full of pitfalls, chiefly in the form of his jealous fiancee!

DOCTOR'S ORDERS by Eleanor Farnes (No. 722)
It was incredible — like a dream. Here she was, in Switzerland, in a world of beauty, luxury and leisure. The events which took place before this lovely fresh Swiss Summer drew to its happy close, were no dream, for Diana, this would last forever . . . .

PORTRAIT OF SUSAN by Rosalind Brett (No. 783)
Managing Willowfield Farm in Rhodesia had made Susan and Paul supremely happy. Then, the owner, David Forrest returned. For her brother's sake, Susan had tolerated his iron-hard selfishness, but how long could her endurance last . . . .

☐ # Volume 22

THE SONG AND THE SEA by Isobel Chace (No. 725)
When Charlotte came from New Zealand to Europe to have her voice trained, she did not expect to find there whom she thought dead, nor to be diving in the Red Sea with him, a charming marine biologist and a beautiful French girl.

CITY OF PALMS by Pamela Kent (No. 791)
On the plane from Paris to Bagdad, Susan had noticed the handsome stranger, with a certain air of aloofness about him. In the emergency which followed, his "aloofness" vanished and he came to her aid, and yet again, in the firghtening wildnerness of the desert . . . .

QUEEN'S NURSE by Jane Arbor (No. 524)
"He has the power to get what he wants", Jess thought bitterly, about this complete stranger. Later, taking up her first "district" as "Queen's Nurse", to her astonishment, she now hoped that this "power" would be directed towards herself!

Golden Harlequin $1.95 per vol.
Each Volume Contains 3 Complete Harlequin Romances

☐ ## Volume 23

A CASE IN THE ALPS by Margaret Baumann (No. 778)
They had always fascinated her, and when the Rilburton family welcomed Katrina into their close-knit and charmed circle, she felt closer to them than ever — Then, she realized, that something was terribly wrong!

THE KEEPERS HOUSE by Jane Fraser (No. 848)
Amabel was resentful that she had to leave her beloved old home and live in a small house on the estate. And even more so, when the new tenant of Kilgenny arrived — a brash young Canadian farmer — this was unbearable!

COME BLOSSOM-TIME, MY LOVE by Essie Summers (No. 742)
Jeannie, her young brother and sister, had escaped a cruel stepfather, and come to the rich farm in New Zealand, where at last, they were happy. Affection was growing too, between Jeannie and her farm manager, until the beautiful, unscrupulous Cecily Chalmers turned up!

☐ ## Volume 28

CITY OF DREAMS by Elizabeth Hoy (No. 542)
Three months in a real Venetian palazzo, working for a real Italian Contessa, and, in the company of Piers Mallory, her most admired Artist! Julie was so excited, but on arrival, she found things quite different . . . not at all as she had expected!

DANGEROUS OBSESSION by Jean S. MacLeod (No. 651)
Faith's fascination for Dr. Maribeau's reputation was so great, that she married him. His insane jealousy soon spoiled their brief happiness, and drove them to exile — then, Grantland Orsett entered Faith's lonely life, only to fan the flame of the Doctor's jealousy yet again!

UNTIL WE MET by Anne Weale (No. 855)
The highly successful star of Parisian cabaret was really, Joanna Allen an ordinary English girl, who longed to settle down and be loved, in her own home. But how could she convince the man she cared for that this was really all that mattered?